MYSTERY
TIMES
TEN

MYSTERY
TIMES
TEN
2011

With Stories By

• Cecila Dominic • Wendy Sparrow • Addie King •
• Johanna Harness • J.A. Souders • Kirsty Logan •
• Elyse Dinh-McCrillis • KC Sprayberry •
• Barb Goffman • Melanie Cummins •

Edited by MaryChris Bradley

Buddhapuss Ink • Edison NJ

Cover and book design by The Book Team

Edited by MaryChris Bradley

Library of Congress Control Number: 2011932397

First Edition

10 9 8 7 6 5 4 3 2 1

ISBN 978-0-9842035-3-6 (Paperback)

First Printing June 2011

Foreword

Buddhapuss Ink was founded with a mission to "put our readers first," and that's just what we did with our first writing competition, Mystery Times Ten 2011. First, all entries had to meet our submission guidelines. They were read and rated by judges from our YA Book Blogger Panel and our YA Teen Panel. The top twenty entries—based on total points accrued—then went on to our Editorial Review Panel, who selected the final ten. We posted our submission call in late 2010.

We weren't sure what kind of response we would get, but in they poured, over two hundred YA short stories by the final deadline. Then it was up to our judges to winnow out the best of this wealth of words.

And winnow they did. They found that some weren't really mysteries, some weren't right for a YA audience, and still others, weren't quite ready for prime time. But oh, the ones they loved were true gems.

To our three panels of judges: We couldn't have done this without you. You were amazing. Slogging through what seemed at times to be an endless pile of stories, you were all diligent, thoughtful, and dead-on in your analysis. Thanks!

To all our entrants we offer a grateful "Thank you!" We enjoyed reading your stories. We laughed, we cried, we were by turns engrossed, scared, and delighted. Well done!

And now, to you—our readers—we hope that you find this year's picks as entertaining and mysterious as we have. You will notice we gave special attention to the top three stories, but to be truthful, we love them all. Thanks for picking up our humble book!

MaryChris Bradley
Publisher, Buddhapuss Ink LLC

Table of Contents

The Coral Temple
by Cecilia Dominic

Lin-Tai swept the sand off the steps leading from the Temple vestibule to the water. She snuck glances at the Sun Dancers as they undulated to the music of the surf and raised their arms to welcome the sunrise. The energy of the moment caught her, and she twirled with a flourish, then gasped at her own audacity. This would not be a morning to be caught distracted. A junior acolyte shirking her duty would be an embarrassment at any time, but especially when the royal family was in residence at their beach castle next to the Temple.

"Do you wish you could join them?"

Lin-Tai looked up from the crack between the flagstones where a few rebellious grains of sand hid from her broom bristles. Princess Rial stood on the top step, arms crossed against the morning's chill. With her dark hair loose around her shoulders and face plain of makeup, she looked like one of the acolytes, only with a fancier robe.

"No, Your Highness. I am happy in my humble work."

The princess laughed. "I saw your little twirl. It's hard not to run down there and join in." She sat on the top step, elbows on her knees and chin on her hands. "Why do you sweep the Temple stairs? The wind will only blow the sand back over them once you finish."

"It is the job of the newest acolyte. I have only been here three weeks. Engaging in this exercise is the first step toward letting go of one's pride and ego." She realized she had stopped sweeping and quickly went back to work. She tried to ignore the sand that seemed to ride on the wind and land on the freshly cleaned surfaces.

"And you get a good view of them." Rial nodded at the dancers, who finished as the lower edge of the sun cleared the water. "Especially the one in the front."

Lin-Tai smiled. "Humble work has its advantages." She had noticed Jor-Gan, senior acolyte and junior dancer, her first day. He executed the steps on the soft sand with ease, the sun silhouetting his lean, muscular body and setting his golden hair aflame.

"What's your name, newest acolyte?"

"I am Lin-Tai." She bowed.

"I like you, Lin-Tai. You're the first one here who's had a conversation with me without sounding like a stuck-up Temple prude."

"You honor me with your words and company, Princess."

"Call me Rial. Oh, here he comes!" She stood and smoothed her robe of seashell-pink silk.

Jor-Gan ascended the steps with sleek grace. Lin-Tai realized her jaw had dropped, and she closed her mouth. Sand crunched between her molars, and she became aware of how grimy she must look next to the princess.

The young man bowed to Rial and turned to Lin-Tai. "The Dance Master would like a word with you."

The broom clattered to the steps. "Me?"

Jor-Gan nodded and picked up the broom. "I'll put this away for you."

"Thank you, Jor-Gan." Lin-Tai bowed to the princess and made her way over the rest of the gritty steps and soft sand to the water's edge, where Dance Master Jalloran stood and watched a circle of junior female dancers rehearse. She could barely make out his features, as he stood between her and the morning sun.

"Ah, Broom-Tai," he said.

Lin-Tai bowed with her palms pressed flat together in front of her chest. She tried not to gasp when a cold wave licked her feet. "You summoned me, Master Jalloran?"

"I have seen you sweeping every day at sunrise," he said without taking his eyes off the slender girls. He winced when one missed a step and stumbled.

Lin-Tai looked at her feet and reminded herself to breathe. Had he seen her that morning, or, she thought, others, when she had danced a few steps as she swept? Would this result in her being dismissed in disgrace?

"Yes, Master. I perform my duties."

"But if the feet want to dance, it is hard not to let them, eh?"

Lin-Tai's throat burned, and she blinked to clear the salt water that had crept into her eyes. "I am sorry, Master. I meant no disrespect."

"It seems, Broom-Tai—what is your real name by the way?—that if the Goddess inspires you to dance, you should do so."

Lin-Tai frowned, not sure whether to respond to the question or the statement. The question seemed safest. "I am called Lin-Tai, Master. And I have always loved to dance."

"Would you like to be a Sun Dancer?"

The energy of the waves and wind made her tingle from head to toe as it echoed her joy. "Oh, Master, more than anything!"

"Then come to the beginner class this afternoon. You need to learn to walk over the sand with grace before you can dance on it." He cringed again as another of the young ladies lost their footing. "As you can see, it's not easy. You are dismissed, Lin-Tai."

She bowed again even though he wasn't looking at her as far as she could tell. He strode over the sand with ease to the circle of young women—who looked less than graceful with sweaty faces and frowns—and barked corrections at them.

Lin-Tai made her way over the sand and back up the stairs to retrieve the broom from the closet at the side of the vestibule's north alcove where Jor-Gan had put it. She reached for the door and then paused. A dark undercurrent rippled through the silent vestibule in spite of the high windows letting in ample sunlight. She closed her eyes and breathed long and deep three times, opening her senses to the sixth degree, and saw the streams of energy as they moved through the Temple, its sanctuary on a cross-point of earth and water. She saw shadows moving, replaying what had happened a few minutes ago. Jor-Gan and the princess had come inside, and she had pushed him against the wall, her lips on his. His arms encircled her, and he clasped the back of her head through her thick hair to bring her closer.

Tears came to Lin-Tai's eyes. Of course he wasn't interested in her. He had only volunteered to fetch her and put away the broom because it would give him an opportunity for time alone with Rial. She shook her head. But that was not the darkness she sensed, as much as it broke her heart. Jor-Gan and the Princess had parted, and he had put away the broom. Lin-Tai saw it then, the sword thrust into his back.

The source of the darkness was the broom closet. She opened it, and Jor-Gan fell out, backward, the tip of the sword sticking through his chest. His landing drove it further through, and fresh blood joined the crusting ooze on the blade.

Lin-Tai screamed and fainted.

• • •

Bitterness in her nostrils and the back of her throat brought Lin-Tai out of the darkness. She coughed and opened her eyes to see Princess Rial's face over her on one side, Master Jalloran's on the other. The Dance Master helped her to sit up and lean against a wall. She tried to bow from her seated position but couldn't stop trembling.

"There, now, Lin-Tai," he said. "It's okay. That was quite the shock."

She tried to speak, but her teeth chattered and her head swirled with the distress of those around her. The vestibule was now filled with people who rushed around, shouted orders, and only contributed to the chaos she felt. She took a couple of deep breaths, drawing energy from the earth through the walls, and calmed herself.

Tears dripped down Princess Rial's cheeks. "Are you all right? I thought you were dead, too!"

Before Lin-Tai could respond, a voice boomed over the chaos. "What is the meaning of this? Where is my daughter?"

Rial rolled her eyes and stood. "I'm here, Father."

Although some of the Royal Guard—not small men—lined the room, the king overshadowed all of them. From Lin-Tai's seated position, he looked like a giant, and she felt his footsteps through the flagstone floor.

"Is this the victim? She looks very alive to me."

"No, Father, she's the one who found him." The Princess' voice broke with suppressed tears. "He's over there." She held a hand out to Lin-Tai and helped her up, keeping her close as they followed the monarch.

The king, who had seen his share of battle wounds, recoiled when he saw the blade sticking out of Jor-Gan's chest. He knelt and touched the bloody tip, rubbing the clotting liquid between his thumb and forefinger. "This is recent."

"Yes, Father," Rial said. "This acolyte and I talked to him just after sunrise."

Lin-Tai noticed that Rial left out the details of the subsequent encounter. Not that she was surprised. The princess wouldn't want her father to know she'd been kissing a lowly Temple dancer, even one as attractive as Jor-Gan.

The king's frown deepened until his black eyebrows had drawn almost entirely together. "Who would cut down a young man like this?"

The doors to the Temple sanctuary flew open, and High Priestess Alara, her cheeks flushed, strode through, followed by the five Vestals who always accompanied her in prayer.

"What is this noise? Who dares disturb my morning prayers?" she demanded, but her hand flew to her mouth when she saw the King. They bowed to each other.

"High Priestess," the king said, "there seems to have been an incident with one of your acolytes." He moved aside to give her a clear view of the body.

"Oh!" Alara swayed, and a Vestal moved to each side of her to steady her. Although the High Priestess had a tendency to be overly dramatic, her appearance alarmed Lin-Tai. Alara's hands had grown so thin they looked like claws, and she had dark circles under her eyes. "How did this happen?"

"I would say that someone stuck a sword in his back."

The king's mouth twitched and Lin-Tai bit her lip to suppress a hysterical giggle. The tension between the monarch and priestess had raised the temperature in the room, and even those who weren't sensitive fidgeted.

"I'm sure it was not one of my Temple personnel," Alara said. "Nothing like this has ever happened, at least not while I have been High Priestess!"

Lin-Tai shivered when she felt a hand on her shoulder. She looked up to see Jalloran. She moved aside so he could pass.

"Sister," he said to Alara, "this is a great tragedy. Young Jor-Gan was one of my better dancers and was on the cusp of starting his Master examination project. We are all feeling his loss."

"And I feel that my family is now in danger," said the King. "We will have to cut our visit short."

"With all due respect, Your Highness," Jalloran replied, "it would likely be best for you and your retinue to stay in residence until this is solved. We have no witnesses, and the murderer may not be with the Temple."

"Just what are you saying, Dance Master? None of my people had anything to do with this!"

"I am saying that we cannot be sure of anything right now," Jalloran replied. "That is a Royal Guard sword sticking out of his back, is it not?"

The king motioned for one of his men to roll the body over and retrieve the sword. It came out with a slick scraping sound and Lin-Tai had to swallow the contents of her breakfast again. The man wrapped the blade in a cloth and handed it to the king, who examined the hilt.

"You are correct, as always, Jalloran."

The Dance Master inclined his head. "Thank you, Your Highness."

"We shall continue this discussion in my conference room at the palace. Rial, back to your rooms! This is no place for a young woman."

"But Father, I want to help with the investigation! Jor-Gan was…" She paused when her father raised an eyebrow. "…a friend, as is this acolyte."

"Very well, she may go with you to comfort you in your loss, but you will stay clear of the Royal Guard as they look into this."

Lin-Tai looked at Jalloran for permission to accompany the princess, but realized she should have been looking at Alara, who now stood with arms crossed and one foot tapping.

"You may go," the High Priestess said. "All classes and activities will be canceled today. We will have a ritual to sing this young man's soul to the Other Side at sunset."

"Thank you, High Priestess."

Lin-Tai bowed and turned to follow Princess Rial out of the side door, but Rial grabbed her hand and pulled her into an alcove that would hide the girls from view while they could watch most of what was happening in the main vestibule. Thankfully, Jor-Gan's body was around the corner.

"He didn't say to go back now!" Rial whispered and put her finger over her lips. "If I'm going to be queen someday, I need to know how to do this!"

Lin-Tai did not say anything. Being close to the princess would help her to determine whether the royal heir had anything to do with the murder. She had been the last person to see Jor-Gan alive, after all. It had nothing to do with Lin-Tai's jealousy, absolutely nothing. The male dancer had just been a fantasy, nothing more.

But her heart broke every time she thought about how she'd never see him dance again and exposed her thoughts as mere rationalizations.

High Priestess Alara retreated back into the Temple to perform a sacrifice for Jor-Gan's soul with her Vestals, and the room cleared out until it was just the king, Jalloran, and a handful of Royal Guard members. The Guards staked out the perimeter and didn't allow anyone in except for the Royal and Temple Physicians—both of whom had been called from their breakfast meeting with local healers—and the Royal Guard captain.

"What is this?" Temple Physician Rolke looked like a frowning vulture most of the time, but his gray eyes darkened when he saw Jor-Gan. "I know this young man."

"How so?" asked the king.

"He was in the Temple Infirmary last week. He said he had tripped down the stairs, banged his knee, and twisted a wrist." He shook his head. "I told him that was rather clumsy for a dancer. Did he say anything to you about it?" he asked Jalloran.

"Nothing," the Dance Master said. "You must've patched him up well. He didn't miss a step in rehearsal."

"He was well-attuned to the water energy, so healing him was no problem."

The king snorted. "Or maybe he just wasn't that badly hurt."

The two physicians shared an exasperated look. Lin-Tai had heard that the king only came to the Temple seasonally to keep up appearances and appease the High Priestess, who had influence over the peasants. She wondered what the high-strung Alara would have said.

"Darandir!" the king said to the Royal Guard Captain.

"Your Majesty!" the captain snapped to attention.

"Check and see if anyone is missing a sword, then report to me in the library at the castle."

"Yes, sire!" He strode out, the guards at the door saluting him as he walked by.

"Well, gentlemen, I'll let you do whatever doctoring things you need to do." The king exited through the front doors followed by the Royal Guard.

Jalloran helped the physicians lift Jor-Gan's body on to a stretcher. It was well known that Temple Physician Rolke had a bad back.

"Shall I help you gentlemen bring him to the infirmary?" asked Jalloran.

"Please." said Rolke. "I must prepare him for the evening ceremony."

They left through the other side entrance, and Lin-Tai exhaled.

"That was interesting." Rial stuck her head out and looked to either side. "I think everyone's gone. What to do now…?"

Lin-Tai crept around the corner, her senses open, but although she could hear the chanting in the Temple, nothing disturbed them. She peeked into the broom closet, but everything was as it should be except for a dark pool on the floor that she ignored. She would probably have to clean it up later, but she was not ritually prepared to deal with blood.

"See anything?" asked Rial.

"No, just…No."

"Good. Then let's go spy on my father in the palace library." Rial led Lin-Tai through the side exit and down the sandstone steps leading to the royal residence. The Coral Temple itself sat at the crest of the bluff, but the Coral Palace still had a nice view of the water to one side and the town to the other. Instead of ascending to the royal chambers when they entered the palace, Rial took Lin-Tai through the kitchen and storage rooms, then up a narrow staircase to the main floor, where they walked down a dark wood-paneled hallway. "This way, no one sees us," the princess whispered.

Lin-Tai heard men's voices and realized that they must be close. Rial tucked her robe around her and lifted a tapestry away from the wall. She squeezed into a two-foot gap that turned into a narrow hallway and ended at a wooden panel.

Rial's breath tickled her ear. "This is a spy hole that I discovered on our last visit here. The servants in the old days would use it so they could anticipate when the king wanted refreshments. No one uses it now except for me; none of the adults can fit."

Lin-Tai reflected that she would probably fit even as an adult, but her frame was narrower than that of the princess, whose womanly figure was just coming into evidence. They pressed their ears to the panel and listened.

"Sit down, Jalloran!" the king said. "You're not going to solve this mess by pacing like a lion."

"I can't help it, Your Majesty." She heard the sound of his body plopping into a wooden chair. "One of my best dancers has been murdered. Plus, I think I just heard something on the other side of that bookcase."

"This place has mice in the walls. I think they chew the corners of the books when we're not here. You know, if you get tired of that Dance Master position, I have one for you back in the Royal Guard."

Lin-Tai raised her eyebrows. She hadn't known that Jalloran had been in the military, and he seemed friendly with the king!

"You honor me with your invitation, but I could never return after having been dismissed in disgrace, even if my name was later cleared. Besides, I'm woefully out of practice with the sword."

"There's brawn and there's brains. You've got the brains, Jalloran, and I need good captains."

"Ah, here's Jor-Gan's roommate. Dal-Gan, please have a seat."

Lin-Tai heard another body sit in a chair, this time more stiffly. She pictured Dal-Gan turning pale under the scrutiny of the king and Dance Master. Like Jor-Gan, he was a junior dancer and senior acolyte.

The king didn't waste time. "When was the last time you saw Jor-Gan alive?"

Dal-Gan's voice quivered. "He's really dead, then? I thought it was a rumor." Dal-Gan sighed deeply. "I last saw him just after rehearsal today when the Dance Master sent him to fetch Broom-Tai."

"And not after?"

"No, Your Highness."

"Did you know of anyone who might wish to hurt him?" asked Jalloran.

"No."

"What about his fall last week, when he visited the infirmary?"

"He said he just fell, but he was coming from the Girls' Quarters. Maybe one of them got jealous and tripped him."

"Is this something he did often?"

Silence.

"Dal-Gan," Jalloran coaxed, "we need to know these things so we can figure out who killed him."

"He would go up once a week to talk with Thea-Gan."

"Who is that?" asked the king.

"Another one of the dancers," Jalloran replied. "She and Jor-Gan had danced as a couple, but any relations beyond the dance are forbidden."

The king chuckled. "Boys will be boys."

"So, did Jor-Gan and Thea-Gan have a relationship?"

Dal-Gan hesitated but finally murmured, "Yes."

Lin-Tai, pressed against Rial in that tight little space, could feel the princess' heart rate speed up, and a warm tear plopped on top of her head.

"I didn't know he had a girlfriend," Rial whispered. "Did you?"

Lin-Tai shook her head. She wondered if Rial had known and had gotten jealous. Or maybe the other girl had. The two men in the library seemed to feel the same, for they then summoned Thea-Gan.

"How long have you been a senior acolyte?" asked the king once she arrived.

"I ascended from Tai to Gan rank last summer, Your Majesty."

"And how long did you know Jor-Gan?"

"Hmmm…I've known him for a few years now. We came to the Temple the same year."

"How long did you have a relationship with him?" asked Jalloran.

"What?" Lin-Tai heard the thump of a fist meeting a chair arm. "Who told you?"

"Well, now that you've confirmed it," the king said, "would you answer the question?"

"We've been seeing each other for about a year. Yes, regularly." Lin-Tai pictured Thea-Gan narrowing her eyes and crossing her arms, as she often did with the junior acolytes. "The only times we didn't see each other was when the Royal Family was here. Then Jor-Gan would disappear."

Rial huffed.

"That's all, Thea-Gan," said Jalloran. "Spend the rest of the day in your room."

"May I at least dance at the ceremony for him?" Now the tears came through in her voice.

"Yes. You are dismissed."

"Well, it sounds like we'd better get my daughter in here," said the King.

Rial and Lin-Tai tiptoed as fast as they could out of the spy hole, and Rial brought them to her rooms. They had just plopped on a chaise lounge when the Royal Guardsman came to get them. He raised his eyebrows, and Lin-Tai realized that both of them had smudged robes and likely dirty cheeks from where they'd pressed them to the wood panel. Rial looked at her and smiled.

"Just you, Your Highness," the guard said when they both got up.

"I'm not going anywhere without my friend."

Lin-Tai shook her head. "That's okay, Princess, I can stay behind."

"No, we're in this together."

When they reached the door, the guard motioned for them to stop. "The High Priestess is in there," he said. "Wait just a moment."

They stood in the hallway, and Rial nudged Lin-Tai closer to the crack in the door, where they could make out the hysterical voice of the High Priestess.

"No, I didn't hear anything!" Alara said. "I was doing my morning prayers with the Vestals."

"The acolyte's scream practically brought the whole Temple to the vestibule, and you didn't hear anything?"

"I was in a deep trance, Jalloran."

"Or still asleep, and you snuck in the back of the Temple with your lazy Vestals when you heard the commotion because you knew you'd look bad."

"I do not have to stay here for this. Let me know when you find the killer. My acolytes are nervous, and I don't know how that will affect the cadet initiation tomorrow."

Lin-Tai looked at the floor as the High Priestess burst from the library. Did that woman ever open a door normally? Lin-Tai suspected that Jalloran's accusations were true. She knew that she hadn't heard any prayers that morning or even sensed any of the energy that should have accompanied them.

"Come in, Rial," the King called.

Rial moved into the library, her hand tightly around Lin-Tai's. "I'm not saying anything without her here."

"Oh, for Goddess' sake, Rial!" The King gestured to Jalloran. "No one's accusing you of anything."

"But you do think I might have had an inappropriate relationship with him."

Lin-Tai closed her eyes. Why didn't the princess just come out and tell the men that they'd been eavesdropping? She'd practically just confessed to it.

"And how would you know that?" Jalloran stood and turned Lin-Tai's face so her cheek and ear caught the light. "It looks like the mice we heard in the walls weren't mice after all."

The king sighed. "This place is riddled with spy alcoves and holes. I thought the Royal Guard had sealed all of them. Now about you and this senior acolyte, Rial..." His voice faded, and Lin-Tai saw the room in negative colors.

Murderer, murderer, murderer, her inner sense told her, and she pulled away from Jalloran and out of the princess' grasp. She saw the sword go into Jor-Gan's back again, but no matter how hard she tried, she couldn't manipulate the vision to see who had done it.

"Lin-Tai?" Rial's voice was tinged with panic. "What is it?"

"I saw the killer's hand for a moment," Lin-Tai whispered and shook her head to clear it. "But I couldn't see the rest of him or her."

"It seems that this acolyte has more ability than our High Priestess," said the king.

Jalloran shot him a sharp look. "Is that true, Lin-Tai? That you have visions?"

She nodded and looked at the floor. "I do, Master. That's why I'm here,.They would come on at home, and some in the village thought I was a witch because I knew things I shouldn't."

"But you couldn't see the murderer. Interesting." The king leaned back and steepled his fingers.

"What are you thinking, Your Highness?" asked Jalloran.

"The mind is a funny thing, Lin-Tai."

Her eyes widened when she realized the king was speaking to her. "Yes, Your Majesty?"

"If your mind isn't allowing you to see something, that's because it doesn't make sense to you for some reason. There's conflicting information it can't reconcile, which means you need more information."

"Then it seems we should let these two participate in our investigation," Jalloran said. "Safely, of course. I'll have my son Lars-Gan accompany them."

Someone knocked on the door, and Royal Guard Captain Darandir entered. He saluted the king.

"You may speak."

"All of the men have their swords, but one of the cadet swords for the ceremony tomorrow is missing."

"And how easy is it to get access to those swords?" asked the King.

"Not too easy, Your Majesty, unless someone wanted to badly enough."

"What is the weight of those swords?" asked Jalloran. "It's been so long I don't remember."

"About three quarters of a Full-Guard sword."

"You will need to correct this lack of security immediately. You are dismissed."

Darandir saluted again and left.

"I thought that sword felt light. That means it's not impossible for a woman to have been the killer. You see what I mean by needing brains?" the king asked Jalloran.

"I'm beginning to, but I don't feel my destiny is back in the Royal Guard, as much as you honor me by your invitation. As for our two mice, why don't you get cleaned up and have lunch, then see what you can find out by talking to the acolytes? Lin-Tai, as a junior acolyte, you should be invisible among the older ones and can eavesdrop. Princess, we know you get along with the boys. See if anyone will tell you anything useful.

I'll let Lars-Gan know that he is to watch out for the two of you. Is this plan amenable to you, Your Majesty?"

"I guess there's no harm in letting them talk to the acolytes," the king replied. "Just no more spying through the walls. And for Goddess' sake, no more kissing in the temple!"

"Yes, Father," said the Princess. Lin-Tai bowed deeply and followed Rial back to the princess' quarters. Soon robes and lunch had arrived for both of them. With clean clothes and faces and full stomachs, they conversed with the acolytes.

• • •

By the time the sun lengthened the shadows on the beach, Lin-Tai and Rial hadn't found out anything interesting, although there was a lot of speculation. Wild theories abounded, including that the high priestess was involved. She wasn't well loved among the acolytes, as they were often called upon to serve her and her lazy Vestals. It was also well known that she often slept through the early prayer time, although there hadn't been any proof until that morning. Jalloran, Lin-Tai was surprised to hear, was also not popular, and there were rumors that he was about to lose his position as Dance Master because of an old scandal, likely the same one he had alluded to with the king. This was mentioned by Dal-Gan when Lars-Gan was distracted talking to the female dancers.

Lin-Tai had kept a close watch on the princess, and although the facts fit—she had a motive, she could have gotten the sword, the weapon was light enough for a female to handle, and Lin-Tai had had that vision when the princess was touching her—she just couldn't be comfortable with the idea of Rial as a murderer. First, the girl had no discretion, so surely she would have slipped and said something. Second, her sadness showed on her face when they were called to prepare for the soul-singing ceremony.

As a junior acolyte, Lin-Tai's job for the ceremony was to chant along with the prayers and keep the candle she held from blowing out in the stiff breeze from the sea. She didn't know the funerary prayers yet, so she hummed along with the melodies and followed the line as it processed into the Temple from the beach, mimicking the path of the sun. The air smelled like tears, and even the features of the Temple facade were lost in the gloom with the setting sun behind it. She thought of Jor-Gan, and how a day that had started with such joy had turned so sorrowful.

He had looked so strong and invincible that morning on the beach. She focused on the candle, and everything clicked into place in her mind.

The Temple facade was blurred because of the light behind it.

Jalloran's face had never been clear to her that morning, and Lars-Gan looked a lot like his father.

Jalloran had been in the military. He would have known where the swords were and how to inflict a fatal wound without the victim crying out.

He had confronted the High Priestess about her laxity, and it was likely he had planted the seed of doubt in the minds of the acolytes.

Jor-Gan had broken the rules and made Jalloran—who had been dismissed from the Guard under suspicious circumstances—look bad. It also made it easy for the Dance Master to frame and punish Thea-Gan, the other offender.

Because he was on the beach every morning, Jalloran could have watched her and known when the vestibule would be empty and unguarded, and it was likely he knew just what she'd do, ensuring that the body would be discovered early and enhancing Alara's appearance of incompetence.

Lin-Tai shook her head. She was grasping at phantoms. There was only one way she could be sure her theory was true and to have more than circumstantial evidence and visions, which could easily be discounted. But why would Jalloran risk everything and expose himself? What if he were next in line to be High Priest, which was possible since Alara was his sister? As High Priest, he would be untouchable for previous offenses in the secular world because he would be seen as Goddess-chosen.

Legend had it that when a new High Priest or Priestess ascended to the Temple throne, the Goddess wrote the name of his or her successor on a scroll kept in a locked room at the bottom of the Temple, forbidden to all but the High Priest or Priestess and the King. This prevented discontented but powerful citizens from "helping" the succession along in return for political favors and influence among the peasants.

Lin-Tai needed to see that scroll.

As the newest acolyte, Lin-Tai was last in line in the procession. She blew out her candle when she passed through the Temple doors and motioned to it when a senior acolyte gestured for her to proceed into the sanctuary.

"Just re-light it off someone else's!" he said.

"It won't. I think there's something wrong with it. I'll duck down to storage and get another one."

"Fine, but hurry!"

Lin-Tai darted down the stairs next to the broom closet and re-lit her candle from one of the torches in a wall sconce. She used its light to guide her down to the catacombs, where Jor-Gan would eventually be buried after his family came and said goodbye. Tears threatened, but she bit her lip and fought them back. She only had a certain amount of time. She focused on her candle flame and imagined what she wanted: the succession scrolls. It illuminated a familiar object in the corner, a broom. She grabbed the broom, holding it in her left hand with the candle, and pulled one of the straws from the bottom, holding it like a dowsing rod.

"Who says country magic doesn't work?" she thought and again focused on the scrolls. The straw held loosely in her right hand swayed, and she followed its implied directions to a locked wooden door with thick metal studs in it. She added a country expletive to the magic. Her foot nudged something on the floor that clinked, and she saw a pair of narrow metal files used to scrape wax drippings from altars and around candles. She used those to pick the lock and let herself into the room.

Scrolls lined the walls dusty shelves, but the ones she wanted were on an altar at the far end of the room. A statue of the three-faced Goddess stood over them, and Lin-Tai knelt before her to ask permission for the transgression she was about to commit.

"The blood of the innocent cries out," came the response clearly in Lin-Tai's head. "The one who was under my protection has forfeited it by murder. But violence begets violence, Little One. Be warned." Lin-Tai saw the murder then from start to finish, how Jalloran had instructed Jor-Gan to fetch Lin-Tai and then had told his son to stay on the beach in his stead. He had walked up to the Temple behind the apprentices and slipped inside behind Jor-Gan and the princess, picked up the sword from where he'd hidden it, and waited for the Princess to leave before stabbing Jor-Gan from behind.

Lin-Tai didn't need to look at the succession scroll. She knew whose name would be on it. She tucked it into her robe and turned to leave, but saw that she wasn't alone.

Jalloran stood in the door and watched her, short sword in hand.

"I can't let you leave with that," he said. "It's against Temple protocol."

Lin-Tai clutched her broom and candle, one in each hand. "It's over, Master Jalloran. You've spilled enough blood today."

"I think not." Jalloran crossed the room, and every time Lin-Tai tried to dart around him, he blocked her. He backed her up against the altar, and she leaned back to avoid the point of the sword.

"Dance," something whispered to her. She didn't have time to think, just held the broom in both hands as she had that morning and twirled. The candle blew out, and she struck something hard—the sword?—with the broom handle and heard it clatter away. Jalloran cursed, and she ducked past him and ran for the door, then down the hallway. Without her dowsing rod, she quickly became lost in the maze-like catacombs.

"Little acolyte!" Jalloran called. "You could die down here, alone in the dark! Why don't you give me what you've taken, and I'll lead you out!"

Lin-Tai remained silent and stilled her breathing. She closed her eyes and prayed to the three-faced Goddess to lead her out. The broom in her hand gave a tug, and although it was dark, she followed it through various twists and turns. It did not lead her back to the Temple, but rather through a passage that smelled like damp earth, and she heard the roar of water. She emerged from a drain pipe that had long been dry and found herself on the beach under the Coral Palace.

With a prayer of thanks, she ran up to the palace and knocked on the door. The Royal Guardsman who had fetched her and the princess earlier let her in.

"I need to speak with the king," she said.

"He is in a meeting with the Royal Captain," the man said.

"Please tell him he was right, and I have the information I lacked. He will understand. By the three-faced Goddess, please!"

After what felt like an hour, but was really no longer than a few long breaths, she was shown in to see the king.

"And what is it that you bring me? A broom?" The king laughed, and she leaned the broom against the door post. "I hear you have information for me."

"The murderer is Jalloran," she said.

The smile disappeared from the King's face. "Jalloran? Do you understand the weight of your accusation, little acolyte?"

"I had a vision, but I'd figured it out for myself first. You were right. I couldn't see him in my vision because I was convinced I'd been talking to him at the time of the murder. I later realized I hadn't seen him clearly because of the sun behind him, and I'd been talking to his son."

"Why would he kill one of his own dancers?"

"Because he wanted to expose Alara as a fraud. What better than a murder and its discovery right outside where she was supposed to be praying so she'd be found out when she didn't emerge to see what was going on?"

"And that would be to his advantage because . . . ?"

Lin Tai took a deep breath and hoped the king would not punish her for criticizing his judgment. "We heard rumors today, Your Majesty, that something horrible happened to one of the Royal Guard trainees when he was Training Master."

"Go on."

"There was an accident during training when Jalloran was supposed to be watching them closely, and the trainee died. He was dismissed and came here, but the scandal followed even though you pardoned him."

"Scandals have a way of doing that, Broom-Tai." The king stood and looked out of the window, where the moon reflected on the crashing waves. "It was fortunate that the scandal re-surfaced at the same time my family was to make its seasonal visit here. Did you happen to find out who had dug it up again?"

"It was Thea-Gan. The boy who died during training was her brother. She had told Jor-Gan and some of the others which undermined Jalloran's discipline and credibility." The king nodded and turned back toward Lin-Tai. "It makes me wonder if Jor-Gan had some help tumbling down those stairs."

"He wants to be High Priest." Lin-Tai pulled the scroll out of her robe. "This is the succession scroll. He's next in line, and he needs protection from the scandal that's about to erupt. That's why you offered to let him back in the Guard, wasn't it, Your Majesty? To let him make things right?"

Now the king's eyebrows threatened to crawl into his hairline. "I've only seen this once, as a young man when it was time for a new High

Priestess to ascend. How did you get it?"

"By the will of the Goddess. She said that he had forfeited her protection by spilling innocent blood, and she warned me that violence begets violence."

"She spoke to you." The king, his face pale, sat back in his chair. "Do you know how long it's been since the Goddess spoke to anyone in the Temple, acolyte or priest? They've all been frauds since, in my opinion."

"I do not, Your Highness, but I do know he killed Jor-Gan."

The doors to the library burst open, but this time it was Jalloran. Lin-Tai winced when the broom clattered to the floor.

"Don't believe a word she says, Your Highness! She's mad!"

"No, she's not!" Rial followed him into the room. Lin-Tai blushed at how she had been trying to pin Jor-Gan's murder on the Princess.

"I have the succession scroll, Jalloran," the king said. "Everything fits into place now."

Jalloran grabbed Rial and held the sword to her throat. "Then I'll just take her." He started backing out of the room.

"No!" The king stood with one arm outstretched. "Leave her alone! Take me instead!"

"A slight girl is easier to handle than a grown man. I'll send her back unharmed if everyone cooperates."

Just then, Jalloran stumbled over the fallen broom. The princess used his disrupted balance to push his sword arm away from her. Two burly Royal Guardsmen pinned him, and Rial ran into her father's arms.

"Throw him in the dungeon." He looked at Rial. "Are you all right, dear daughter?"

"I'm fine, Father." She gestured to Lin-Tai. "Are you okay?"

"I think so." Lin-Tai plopped into the chair a Guardsman placed behind her. "It's been a strange day, Your Highness, Princess."

"It's only going to get stranger," said Rial. "During the ceremony for Jor-Gan, Alara had a fit and is unconscious. The Temple physician says she may not last the night. I was coming to tell you, Father, so you could get the succession scroll."

"Jalloran is her successor," the king said. "Or was. He forfeited his right of ascension when he killed the acolyte. It's ironic he didn't wait." He glanced at the scroll, and his eyes grew wide. "We need a new High Priestess, and as I said, it has been generations since the Goddess has spoken or since the High Priest or Priestess has demonstrated a talent for vision."

"Oh, Lin-Tai, look!" Rial said and pointed to where the scroll lay open on the table. Faded script that grew darker by the second appeared beneath Jalloran's name: Linora.

"I can't be the High Priestess! I'm a junior acolyte!"

"It is the will of the Goddess," said the king. "Do you accept?"

Lin-Tai stood and bowed to the king. "I accept." She felt Rial by her side and hugged her friend, whom she would never doubt again.

High Priestess–elect Linora felt the energies of the air, water, earth, fire, and spirit wash over her, and when she closed her eyes, visions crowded around her. One, of Jor-Gan dancing in the moonlit surf, brought tears to her eyes. He turned, bowed to her, and said, "Thank you!" before fading into the waves.

Cecilia Dominic supports her writing habit through the practice of clinical health psychology and behavioral sleep medicine. She lives in Atlanta, Georgia with her husband and two cats. She is on the board of the Village Writers Group and is a member of the Romance Writers of America and Georgia Romance Writers. For fun, she blogs about wine, food, and life at random-oenophile.blogspot.com and about writing at ceciliadominic.blogspot.com.

• Second Place •

Passing Notes

by Wendy Sparrow

Life didn't begin or end when you received a note from a guy you liked, unless you were Brigit Masterson, and even she didn't quite manage to kill herself. The doctors said she'd be okay eventually. They still had her in the ICU, and Chloe and I wouldn't be able to talk to her for a while. They wouldn't let us visit.

The only reason I knew about the note was because I'd found Brigit with that note in her hand and the bottle beside her. If Brigit wasn't so effing impulsive *and* she'd stopped to think it over, she'd have known that no guy, especially not a guy who would blackmail you, is worth that. Brigit was always doing stuff like that though, leaping first and thinking later. It was probably how she wound up clutching a note that said, "Don't tell anyone or I'll tell your parents what we did after the party."

It wasn't signed, but a guy had written it, and I'd pocketed it. Yeah. That was dumb. Pocketing evidence wasn't one of my brighter moves.

Brigit was the impulsive one, and the party girl.

Chloe was the beautiful one.

Me, Alexis, I was the one who wanted to find out who'd done this to Brigit.

• • •

I cornered Chloe outside under the big oak during lunch the next day. She'd know more about the party than I would. I'd stayed home and worked on this stupid paper for my history class last Friday night. Well, okay, the paper wasn't stupid, and I probably wouldn't have been allowed to go to Trey Walker's party anyway. My parents are a little uptight. They would have drilled me on who was going to be there and whether there'd be alcohol. I can lie to a lot of people, but not my parents. Once they'd found out Brigit was going to be there, they'd have known what kind of party it was.

"Who was at the party Friday night?" I asked Chloe.

Chloe was always on some new fad diet even though she was already skinny. This time it was some new whole-grains diet, so she was eating something freaky that, I swear on my soul, looked like raw seeds. Mm okay...I bet that'd have her running for the girls' bathroom later.

"A lot of people." She was sipping water in between each swallow. Those seeds looked completely unappetizing. At least her raw fruits and veggies diet hadn't required her to drown her taste buds between bites.

I pulled out my notepad. "Guys, Chloe. I need to know which guys were there, and only the guys Brigit was interested in. Who was there?"

She slid another mouthful of dry seeds into her mouth as she tilted her head up to the sky to consider this. "Hmm. There was Luke. That foreign exchange student from Denmark...whatever his name is. Ethan. Oh, you know who was there that really surprised me? Cooper."

"Cooper? The guy she got suspended last year?"

Brigit should have been suspended right along with Cooper, because they'd both swiped the answer sheet from Ms. Knight's desk, but Cooper had taken the blame for it. In fact, Brigit had gotten an A on that test, and Cooper, poor goofy guy, had wound up home for two days, with a nasty mark on his previously perfect, geeky record.

"What was Cooper doing there?" I put a star next to his name.

Chloe smiled around the spoon in her mouth. "He wanted to be doing Brigit, but she was more interested in Ethan." That made sense— Cooper had a crush on Brigit. He always had. It was why he'd taken the blame for her. Still, he wasn't the type of guy to go to a party like the one Friday night. Why had he been there?

"That's it? That's the guys there she might have been interested in?"

"Or who might have been interested in her...yeah. I haven't figured out how she feels about Cooper." Chloe bit her lip and blinked. Her eyes looked shiny like she was about to cry. I'd cried myself ugly the previous day. "She's going to be okay, right, Alexis?"

I nodded. "Totally. I was going to call and check in with her parents after school, but her mom told me this morning the doctors said she'd be fine."

I fingered the note in my pocket. I'd shoved it there when I'd found Brigit out cold on the floor in the bathroom off her room. It seemed wrong to let whoever had written the nasty note win by virtue of her parents finding it. Brigit really would have thought better of taking all those pills if she'd given it a bit of time.

Pulling out the note, I showed it to Chloe. "Do you recognize the handwriting on this?"

Chloe's brown eyes widened to the size of quarters. "That's what happened?"

"Don't tell anyone! But do you recognize the handwriting? I want to know who did this to Brigit."

Chloe shook her head so fiercely that her braided, brown hair smacked her cheek. "It's a guy's handwriting, though."

Yeah, that much was obvious. No girl would write like that. Not in a million years.

"Did anything happen at the party that night, Chloe? Or did you see Brigit leave with anyone?"

Chloe took a long drink from her water bottle while she thought it over. "I was busy hanging out with Tyson." She rolled her eyes. "He kept trying to get me to take a sip of this beer he'd swiped because he wanted to see if I'd hurl. I wasn't paying that much attention to Brigit. She was still there when I made Tyson take me home at one. My parents flipped out that I was that late. My curfew is eleven now. Eleven!" Eating another gob of seeds, she wrinkled her nose in a grimace. I wasn't sure if it was over the new curfew or those nasty seeds.

"What is that crap you're eating?" I asked her, putting away my notebook.

"Wheatberries. You want some?"

"Not even a little bit."

I decided to talk to the foreign exchange student first. I had Cooper in one of my classes, so he'd be easy enough to corner. Besides, I'll admit it, I sorta thought Anton was cute. He was only going to be here for another semester before he went back to Denmark. I'd thought everyone from Denmark had blonde hair, but Anton had really dark brown hair that was curly. I sat behind him at an assembly once, and I'd spent the whole time wishing I was brave enough to run my fingers through his hair. It looked so soft. I wasn't the flirt, though...that would be Brigit or even Chloe, not me. Anton had dark brown eyes too. It just blew away all my ideas of what people from other countries were supposed to look like.

He was sitting on the steps with his phone out, texting or tweeting or something.

"Hey, Anton," I said when I was about six feet away.

He looked up, blinked once, and a wide smile slid across his face, making two dimples appear in his cheeks. Whoa. He had dimples? I'd never noticed that.

"Hey, Alexis." He put his phone in his pocket. Just like that, I crossed him off my list. I mean, we'd spoken a dozen times maybe, and he put his phone away to talk to me? A guy who did that would never blackmail Brigit. There was just no way.

I sat down on the steps next to him, still bathing in the glow from that smile of his. He was smiling at me, and he was from Denmark, and he was so cute.

"How is your friend—uhh—Brigit?"

See? He'd asked about her. It wasn't him. I knew it wasn't him, but he might be able to help me figure it out.

"The doctors said she's going to be okay, and that's sorta what I wanted to talk to you about."

"It is?" He raised his eyebrows in surprise. Even his eyebrows were cute. He picked up a soda and sipped from it. It was totally distracting. I couldn't seem to focus beyond the sight of his lips wrapped around the straw. He had a tiny scar in the corner of his mouth that had faded to just a white line, but it seemed to say to me, "Here, Alexis. You really want to kiss him here."

I really did.

Blinking myself out of my stupor, I asked, "Uhh, yeah, I know something that happened Friday night is the reason why Brigit did what she did, and I want to find out, you know? Chloe said you were at the party."

His eyebrows drew together. I could have sat there for hours watching expressions chase across his face. Were all guys in Denmark this hot? Probably not, but maybe. "I was there, but I never spoke with Brigit. She spent all her time with…" He closed his eyes and tapped a finger on his leg. "I'm not so great with names. He is really tall. I think he is on the soccer team or something."

"Ethan?"

"Yes," he said, opening his eyes.

I wanted to write that down, but it would probably look really dorky. Chloe was used to me writing notes to myself but, yeah, I could just remember it this time. Besides, this way I could stare at Anton while I thought that over.

Brigit kept telling me she didn't like Ethan anymore in that way, but if she'd spent all her time with him at the party, maybe she'd changed her mind. They used to be together. Brigit said she didn't like how jealous he always was, and he had a nasty temper. If she was honest with herself, he was a little too much like her, but Brigit probably wouldn't see that. Not that Brigit had a temper, but she did get really emotional fast, and then it'd blow through like a phase.

So was she with Ethan or not? Hmm.

Ethan was sort of hot if you weren't spending time with a foreign exchange student who was fifty times hotter. Brigit had been interested in Anton when he'd first arrived, but she said he seemed too smart for her.

That was a big thing with Brigit; she was really self-conscious about things, so she didn't want any guy who was too much of anything.

Then again, she'd hung out with Cooper a few times, and he was smarter than the entire senior class combined. Maybe she just felt sorry for him on account of him getting in trouble for her and everything. I mean, it wasn't as if Cooper had needed those answers. He'd have blown through the test if he'd been allowed to take it.

"You weren't at the party," Anton said. "I looked for you."

"You did?" My stomach was all giddy and sick at the same time. He'd looked for me at the party?

He nodded and smiled so that his dimples appeared again.

"My parents don't let me go to parties like that," I said.

"Do your parents let you go see movies on school nights?"

"Uhh..." I had no idea. My parents wouldn't know what to think probably. The guy I used to date, well, we'd just always hung out at someone's house. We didn't really date because he was saving his money for a car.

Anton winced. "I'm so sorry. What am I thinking? You're probably worried about your friend. Perhaps, if you're not doing anything this weekend?"

I loved how deliberate every word he said was. I figured it was because English was his second language. Still, it was like he tasted every word first to make sure it was the right one before he said it. It was hot. He didn't have much of an accent. I'd heard that his family travelled a lot so maybe he wasn't originally from Denmark. That would explain the dark hair maybe. Maybe I just didn't know enough about Denmark.

"Okay," I said. That was much easier to answer.

"Saturday? I can borrow my host family's car, and we can go out to dinner and to see a movie. If that's okay?"

It was so, so, so okay.

"Okay," I said again. Oh, geez, Alexis! Prove to him that you have a bigger vocabulary than one word. "So…uhh…nothing happened at the party that you saw?"

"I was there with my host brother James, and we left at around eleven." His smile was all lopsided as he leaned toward me. "I think we might have been the first to leave, but I was bored."

"You were bored?" He'd been bored…at one of Trey's parties. That just never happened. What kind of wild parties did they hold in Denmark?

Anton shrugged. "There wasn't anyone there I was interested in." He was staring right at me, and he smiled a two-dimpled smile again.

I was so glad the bell rang right then because my face flushed bright red, and I probably would have said "okay" again…and again…and again. He was so okay.

"Can I get your phone number?" he asked.

Of course! It was perfect. I couldn't rule him out officially, even if my heart and head already had, until I'd checked if he'd written the note.

"Sure. Can I get yours? And your email address?" His email address would have letters in it. Sometimes I was just ridiculously smart.

Another two-dimple smile from Anton. I felt guilty being so happy with Brigit in the hospital. It felt wrong to be happy. I'd really try to stop that after I'd left Anton. I pulled out my notebook and carefully skipped the page with his name on it. A moment later, we'd traded pieces of paper, and I'd tucked his folded note into my pocket as I ran to my locker.

When I could hide a quick glance at it, I yanked it out. I didn't even need to pull out the other note to compare; there was no way they were a match. Anton hadn't written the note to Brigit. Even though I'd never thought it was him, I breathed out a sigh of relief before I yanked out books for my next class.

Cooper was twirling a gold dollar on the desk in front of him when I sat down beside him. He glanced up with a frown that only deepened when he saw me.

"What's wrong? Is she okay? She's okay, right?" he asked me. Even when he was talking I could see the lines in his cheeks from his frown. Had he been frowning all day? It looked like it. His jaw looked tight, and his eyes were pinched in the corner with strain. Cooper was an intense guy. He seemed like he cared, though. But maybe he just didn't want anyone to find out what he'd done. Cooper wasn't as easy to read as other guys because you could just tell he had like twenty thoughts for each one of yours.

"The doctors said she is going to be okay."

He relaxed, slightly. Honestly, Cooper scared me a little. He really, really liked Brigit, and I worried about what he might do if he thought he didn't have a chance with her. He was a bit of a geek, and she was, well, Brigit. The only reason they were friends was because his parents and her parents were friends. They went to the same church or something. Brigit had gone on a couple dates with Cooper that had almost seemed like pity dates; even though she'd said they'd had fun. He was too nice. Brigit never went for guys that were too nice.

It wouldn't be easy to ask Cooper questions without him getting suspicious. I mean, he might have passed her the note yesterday at school. He did know her parents, so he'd know also that threat would work on Brigit.

Of course, most of the seniors knew that Brigit kept things from her parents. Brigit was always telling her parents she was somewhere with other people when she was really at a party. I can't tell you how many times she'd said, "If my parents ask, I was with you." I was really glad her parents never thought to ask me. I don't think I could lie to her parents any more than I could lie to my own.

"I thought that when you sat next to me, you were going to tell me that she'd died or something." Cooper had gone back to spinning his dollar. It was hypnotizing to watch the coin spin.

I swallowed. Maybe I could be honest. Well, sort of honest.

"I found her yesterday. It was...it scared the crap out of me." I glanced up at the teacher. It was easy to talk in American Lit because Mr. Henley took like half the class to take roll. Still, I lowered my voice. Brigit wouldn't want everyone hearing this, and I didn't want to admit to how dumb I'd acted. "When I found her, I thought she was dead. I couldn't tell if she was breathing...and..." I took a deep breath. "It was awful. I've never been so scared. I couldn't move. I just stood there, shouting her name. Stupid, huh?"

Cooper shook his head.

"The doctors said she'd be okay, though. I think they might just be keeping her because they're worried about her."

"Why would she do it?"

His eyes looked honest. You can read a lot in a person's eyes, and I just wasn't seeing anything other than gut-wrenching worry in Cooper's. He really, really liked Brigit. It was the perfect chance for me to ask questions. Cooper may have been the only one at the party with his eyes glued to Brigit.

"I think something happened at the party on Friday."

Cooper glanced away and down at his book.

Okay, so maybe I was wrong. He looked guilty again.

"Did something happen at the party, Cooper?"

He slid his notebooks into his bag. "You don't want to know."

"I do. I'm worried about Brigit."

"Brigit wouldn't want you to know, okay? Trust me on this." He raised his hand. "Mr. Henley, I feel sick. Can I go to the nurse's?"

A minute later, he was gone. So much for that. He'd put his notebooks away so fast that I didn't even get a chance to see if his handwriting matched.

The last two guys on my list could always be found together. Luke and Ethan were best friends and both on the soccer team. Instead of heading home to work on homework, I stashed all but my notebook in my car and went out to watch soccer practice. The soccer team had its own groupies so I wasn't the only one out there, but I'm not much into sports so Ethan noticed me right away.

When they broke for a moment, he ran over to the fence I'd been watching through. "Hey, Alex. I heard Brigit's going to be okay."

The whole school had been talking about Brigit. I wasn't sure what

Brigit would think of that when she came back. Brigit liked attention, but probably not this kind. I hadn't been the one to tell everyone. Brigit lived next to Becky Turner. Once Becky Turner knew something, you might as well just put it in the school newspaper.

"Yeah, I heard you and her were together again, so I thought maybe you'd know why she did it." I hadn't heard that, but I'd watched enough cop shows to know that sometimes you made statements just to see if they'd contradict you.

Ethan sneered and looked angry. "You heard that, huh?" He glanced over his shoulder at Luke. "She wasn't with me...not in the end."

Uhh okay. "Everyone said you guys were together at the party."

Ethan rolled his eyes and tipped his head back as he hung on the chain-link fence between us. His knuckles were white as he gripped the chain-link. "Well, they didn't get to see the show after the party, so they wouldn't know." When his head tipped down and he looked at me, he looked sad more than angry. What had happened after the party? Ethan glanced over my shoulder and glared. "What's up, freak? You got something to say?"

I turned around. Cooper was there.

"I'm just here to talk to Alexis," Cooper said. He glared back at Ethan.

"You think you're all bad-ass now, huh?" Ethan's nostrils flared as he said this. It was not a good look for him.

Luke glanced at our group before jogging over.

"What's going on?" Luke was staring at Cooper. He wasn't mad like Ethan. I couldn't tell what he was feeling. Being in the middle of this was starting to sound like one of my dumb ideas...almost as dumb as grabbing that note.

"Haven't you done enough?" Ethan swiveled his head to look at Luke. I'd never seen the two not getting along. They'd been best friends for years.

"I should go." I gestured behind me.

Luke had switched to staring at Ethan, and he said quietly to me, "Yeah, you should. Tell Brigit we're glad she's okay."

Ethan punched Luke in the shoulder. "You don't speak for me. There is no 'we', bro."

As Ethan walked off, Luke smiled tightly at me. "Sorry, Alex. You should go." He went back to practice too, rubbing his shoulder where Ethan had punched him.

Cooper walked me to my car silently, but when I turned to ask him what he'd wanted to speak with me about, he was already twenty feet from my car, walking away.

• • •

It seemed like everyone liked to pass notes, because I got one in my locker the next day. The handwriting was different from the writing on Brigit's, but it felt just as threatening. "Keep out of it!"

"Have you heard anything new?" a guy asked behind me.

I turned and smiled when I saw it was Anton. I shouldn't be this happy…not after getting my own note.

"New?"

"About your friend." His eyes were all soft and warm with concern. There was just no way he'd sent either note.

"Her parents said she is going to be fine, and she might go home soon. They just want to watch her and talk to her, I guess. I'm hoping to go see her sometime this weekend."

Her mom had sounded exhausted on the phone, so I hadn't wanted to push for any sooner or ask many questions. Brigit could be somewhat self-destructive, but they'd never really seen that side of her. They didn't even know about the thing with Cooper. This had probably been a painful slap of reality for them.

"That's good," he said.

"I still wish I knew what happened. I don't want her doing it again, and Brigit just sometimes does stuff without thinking." It was a bit of an understatement, but Anton didn't know Brigit well enough to know that.

"No luck figuring it out?"

I thought of the note in my locker. I'd annoyed someone and found out that Ethan was pissed at the world, but I couldn't count that as progress.

"Not really. Ethan mentioned that something happened after the party, but he wouldn't say what, and he and Luke seem to be fighting."

"Luke is…?"

"The blonde-haired guy on the soccer team who's always with him. They were best friends."

"Not anymore?" Anton's eyebrows rose at the question, and I just

wanted to sit and stare at him instead of talking. Anton probably wasn't
the cutest guy in the school, but the way he moved and talked and the
way he was made him the cutest—if that makes sense.

I shrugged. "It doesn't seem like it."

Anton glanced over my shoulder. "Uhh...you're not with someone,
right?"

"With someone?" I was standing here talking to him, but that much
seemed obvious.

"You don't have a boyfriend?"

I frowned at him. Really? He had to ask that after I'd agreed to go on
a date with him on Saturday?

Anton's cheeks went pink when he saw my expression. "Sorry. No.
Of course not. It's just. Never mind. Forget I asked that." He glanced
over my shoulder again.

The bell rang just as I turned to see who he was looking at. Everyone
in the corridors moved all at once blocking my view. Crap. I'd seen someone out of my periphery, and it had felt like someone was staring at the
back of my head.

"I'll see you later, Alexis," Anton said, and he was gone too.

So I'd managed to have an awkward conversation with the guy I
liked, get my own threatening note, and I was nowhere closer to solving
the mystery of who'd sent Brigit hers. I was off to a great start on my
Wednesday. Hopefully the ceiling would fall on my head and really make
this day special.

I pulled out my note again and stared at it, willing a name to appear
at the bottom. The handwriting was neat and exact. It was cramped and
stilted in that special way that only guys can manage. A satisfied smile slid
across my face as it occurred to me that it was written on graph paper.
Sure, most of the students in the junior and senior classes had graph paper
in one of their binders, but, really, only a guy would use it for a note.

Cooper was at his locker when I got there, and he was staring into it
as if something had come to life inside. Hopefully nothing had, but he
was really into science, so you never knew.

"Cooper?"

He jumped and looked at me. His skin was so pale. Geez, he looked like he'd seen a ghost. I moved to his side and stared at whatever horror was in his locker. He'd gotten a note too…and it wasn't on graph paper.

"Shut your mouth or I'll kill you," I read over his shoulder in a whisper.

Holy freak! It was in the same handwriting as Brigit's had been. Cooper crumbled the note into a ball and darted looks around him.

Grabbing his arm, I dragged Cooper outside. We'd both be late to class, but I didn't care. First period was less important than finding out who was sending these notes. I mean, I still thought Cooper had sent me mine, but he was officially off my list for Brigit's note. Nothing crossed you off the list as fast as getting your own note…and his was scarier than Brigit's, in my opinion. It also meant he knew what was going on. He had to; otherwise, why send him a note? No, he knew.

I pulled him out underneath the oak tree where I had talked to Chloe.

"What's going on, Cooper?"

"I'm not going to tell you."

Some of the paleness had receded in his cheeks and a stubborn expres-sion had settled in. I hate stubborn guys. They can be such a pain. Not that I want a guy who lets you push him around, but Cooper had to understand we had to get this out in the open, didn't he?

"Brigit got a note too." I dug the note out of my pocket and waved it under his nose.

Cooper snatched the small piece of paper from my fingers and read it. "This is why? This is why she did it?"

"Yes, and I'm not going to let someone get away with threatening Brigit."

Cooper shook his head and handed the note back with a sigh. "No, I know. We should tell…someone."

"What? What should we tell them?"

Sticking both his hands in the pockets of his jeans, Cooper started to pace. "At the party…well, when it was ending, Ethan caught them, but you know Brigit…she didn't mean it. I think she might have been drinking."

"What did Ethan catch them doing?"

Cooper rolled his eyes with a grimace. "Ethan caught Luke and Brigit

...going at it...and he was just...pissed. He yelled all these horrible things at her.""In front of everyone?" Wow! How had I not heard about this? No wonder Brigit was such a mess.

"No, it was in one of the back rooms. I'd gone to check on Brigit because she'd disappeared, and the party was breaking up. I didn't want her driving home like that because she just looked...like she shouldn't be driving. Most everyone who stayed that long shouldn't have been driving. I figured the least I could do was drive her home. So, I walked in and told Ethan to lay off her, and he told me to mind my own business before he slammed by me, and we heard him gun his engine outside."

"That's what this is all about?" All these notes? All this drama? Brigit had nearly died because she'd gotten smashed and tried to hook up with her semi-boyfriend's friend? Really?

Cooper swallowed and shook his head. "No, Brigit freaked out and asked me to drive behind Ethan to make sure he made it home. Luke hadn't been drinking, so he said he'd do it, but Brigit insisted. So, I followed Ethan's car with Brigit. Ethan totally shouldn't have been driving. He was all over the road. I kept honking the horn and trying to get him to stop."

We'd still been somewhat visible from the inside of the school...that had been my first mistake. The front door to the school was yanked open, and Ethan stormed outside. I'd thought Ethan was mad the day before. Holy freak! His face was red and blotchy and both his hands were already clenched into fists. Luke followed him out the door a moment later.

My second mistake was thinking I could handle this. Ethan was pissed.

Cooper, hearing the noise and seeing my shocked face, turned to see them approaching.

"Shut up, Cooper!" Ethan shouted.

"You shouldn't have been driving!" Cooper shouted back.

Ethan tackled Cooper, dragging him down into the grass. He punched him right in the face. I screamed—and not in a quiet way, either. I mean, I really, really screamed.

Luke dove on top of them and tried to yank Ethan away as Cooper swung a punch that was much harder and nastier than I would have guessed quiet and geeky Cooper had in him. It made a squelching sound when it connected with Ethan's nose. It was so gross. Blood just spurted everywhere.

The door opened again. Anton looked out, and his mouth dropped open as he watched the three guys wrestling at my feet under the oak.

"Get someone!" I yelled to Anton.

He nodded and bolted back inside.

I wanted to stop the fight, but both Ethan and Cooper just kept throwing wild punches. I didn't want to get anywhere near their fists. Ethan's nose was just spraying everything with blood, and Cooper was going to have a fat lip and probably a black eye.

Cooper yelled, "You didn't even stop after you hit that car, Ethan!"

"Shut up! Just shut the hell up! It's none of your business. Do you hear me? None of your freaking business!"

Every time Luke would manage to get Ethan pulled off of Cooper, Cooper would just take the opportunity to pound his fists on Ethan's face.

"Stop it! Stop it, both of you!" I screamed.

Then Anton was back with teachers, and Anton had his arm around me and was pulling me out of the way as Mr. Carpenter, the band leader, grabbed Cooper.

"You shouldn't have been driving!" Cooper yelled at Ethan. "You shouldn't have sent Brigit the note! It's your fault that she tried to kill herself!"

Ethan was wiping the blood from his mouth and panting while Luke held him back. "What?" he asked, squinting. He spit a mouthful of blood onto the grass. "What the hell are you talking about?"

It was quiet, aside from their breathing and the door slamming open as more adults from the school came to deal with the fight.

"I sent the notes," Luke said.

My mouth dropped open. I'd assumed it was Ethan. No, it *had* to be Ethan. That was like Ethan. He was violent, and as impulsive as Brigit. Ethan was trying to cover up some hit-and-run on Friday night. That's what this was about.

"This whole thing was my fault. I knew what I was doing. I shouldn't have touched her. I knew how Ethan would take it. It was stupid." Luke ran a hand through his hair and clenched his teeth while closing his eyes. "I sent them."

. . .

They didn't let Brigit go home until Saturday morning. They had her under observation, her mom said. Her mom kept telling me Brigit was going to be getting the help she needed…over and over. I didn't say it, but I kinda thought not having Luke and Ethan at the school messing with Brigit's head would help quite a bit too. They were both in so much trouble.

There was already a car in front of Brigit's house when I got there. I had a few hours before my date with Anton, so I figured I'd stop by and see her. I didn't recognize the car, so it wasn't Chloe's.

Her mom let me in. "She's downstairs watching TV."

I was halfway down the stairs when I heard them talking, and I stopped.

"You scared me to death, Brigit," Cooper said. His voice sounded so different from the last time I'd heard him. He'd gotten suspended again, this time for fighting. Brigit's influence sure hadn't been good on his record. Even though I couldn't see them, I knew Cooper looked like he'd been in a fight from seeing him on Friday. He had two black eyes and a split lip. I suspected, though I didn't know, that Ethan had looked worse. "I can't believe you did this over a note. I wouldn't have let anything happen to you."

Okay, Cooper got props for that, and I couldn't help smiling.

"I know," she said. "It was stupid. I didn't think. I just freaked out."

"Promise you won't ever do that again. You can just talk to me, you know? Never again, Brigit."

My heart went "awww," and I started quietly back up the stairs.

Brigit's voice sounded all soft and shy when she answered. "No…it was stupid. What happened with Luke…"

"That doesn't matter to me."

"Well, that was stupid too. It didn't mean anything, Coop, I swear it didn't. I don't even like him that way. I don't know what I was thinking." That was Brigit for you. Too impulsive.

It was sweet that she called him "Coop." It sounded dumb, which was what made it sweet.

I'd underestimated Cooper. He might seem goofy and all, but he really seemed to love Brigit. He'd fought for her and got suspended for her. Twice.

"You look like you got hurt pretty bad in that fight," Brigit said.

"You should have seen Ethan." He sounded so proud when he said it. I had to respect that, and he did fight like a street fighter—which was weird for a guy who wrote notes on graph paper. "He's never going to bother you again, I swear, Brigit."

It sounded like they were kissing, so I backed up the rest of the steps. I didn't want to intrude on that. That would be weird on so many levels.

Brigit's mom gave me a funny look when she saw me at the top of the stairs.

"I'll come back tomorrow," I said.

Her mom smiled. She probably had already figured out Cooper might be good for Brigit. Maybe he'd keep her from doing stupid things and being impulsive.

I still had a cheesy smile on my face when I got back into my car, and it didn't dim when I looked down at the note on the passenger seat. It had been underneath the windshield wipers of my car after school yesterday.

It was in a guy's handwriting and it wasn't signed, but I had a good idea who it was from.

"I can't wait to see you tomorrow night. I can't stop thinking about you. I hope you like Thai food."

Life didn't begin or end when you got a note from a guy you liked… but it felt pretty amazing if you ask me.

Wendy Sparrow spends most of her free time imagining how to get her characters out of the horrible situations she's dumped them in. When that gets dull, she parents two quirky kids with autism and glamorously washes laundry for her loving and supportive husband. She can often be found on Twitter spouting Mountain Dew–fueled opinions or in her "office"—the corner of the couch—typing away on her next YA novel.

• Third Place •
Poltergeist on Aisle Fourteen
by Addie King

I didn't hear chains rattling. I didn't trip on slimy ectoplasm or notice cold pockets of air as I walked through the store.

But he was there just the same.

Dayton, Ohio isn't a hotspot for supernatural activity. If I had been looking for ghosts, I would have checked out the mortality challenged in a voodoo cemetery in New Orleans, or at that house in Amityville. I'm not a ghost hunter though. I'm Julianna Kent, a seventeen-year-old high school senior and cheerleader. I've always believed in ghosts, but I never expected one to dog me down the produce aisle at Kroger's.

Grocery runs can be an adventure. Mom works nights, so she gives me the money and I end up doing the grocery shopping on my way home from practice or a basketball game. I also do the cooking, so she will have something to eat when she gets home.

I'm not an organized shopper with a coherent list and a pack of coupons. This has resulted more than once in overbuying toilet paper or forgetting to buy milk, but I enjoy the excitement of creating meals on the fly. Tonight, nothing in the fridge sounded good, which is why I was in Kroger's after cheerleading practice.

I was halfway through the fresh produce, right between the Yukon Gold potatoes and the Vidalia onions, when I felt something small and soft hit the back of my head. I reached up to touch the spot and it was wet. When I looked at my fingers, they were covered in a red mush. I knew it wasn't blood when I saw the seeds.

Just as I realized I'd been hit with an overripe strawberry, I was hit again, this time with a grape. I turned around and saw a teenage stock boy, busily fussing with a display of tangerines. It had to be him. There weren't a whole lot of other people around. He was directly behind me, at a perfect angle to lob fruit at the back of my head.

"What do you think you're doing?" I asked.

He shook his head and looked down at the floor. His shoulders slumped for a moment. There was something off about him, but I couldn't quite put my finger on what.

I marched up to him, my hands on my hips, and channeled my best impression of my mother when I landed in hot water. This little punk had gotten strawberry mush in my hair. I had just gotten highlights. They were expensive, and I wouldn't have any spare cash in my budget for the next month because of them. If he didn't have a good excuse, I would absolutely complain to the manager.

His face lifted to mine as I walked toward him. His deep brown eyes opened wide as he stared at me.

"What, are you surprised you got caught?" Now I was angry, at least until another shopper walked right *through* him. To my chagrin, it was our next-door neighbor, Howard Jameson, a sweet old man who had taken it on himself to watch over me. I thought of him as a substitute grandfather, since my own had died when I was eight.

"Julianna Kent, what's the matter with you?" He put an arm around my shoulders, guiding me away from the staring shoppers.

I couldn't turn away; I kept staring at that stockboy even as I responded to Mr. Jameson. "I'm sorry, sir, but someone threw a strawberry at my head." I showed him the seeds on my fingers.

He escorted me over to the manager, gently admonishing my outburst and yammering on about knowing the proper way to deal with a complaint. The young stock boy followed us, and that was when I realized he wasn't walking; he was floating. I couldn't help but watch him even as Mr. Jameson muttered about young people overreacting to small annoyances. I wondered if going insane counted as a small annoyance. When we found a manager, I showed him the seeds.

"Ma'am, I'm awful sorry about what happened. Do you know who it was?" He was making notes on a clipboard.

"Well, he's five-ten, about eighteen years old, African American, with a scar on his right cheek." It wasn't hard to describe him; I was staring right at him. He still looked surprised. I don't know why. Didn't he expect to get in trouble for what he'd done? I'm just not quite sure how Mr. Jameson had managed to walk right through him. Someone must be playing a practical joke.

The manager's mouth formed a little "o" as the clipboard slid from his hands and fell to the floor with a clatter. "We—we don't have anyone working here by that description any longer."

I wanted to call him on it, but the stock boy put one finger to his lips and shook his head. A moment later, the manager picked up his clipboard and told me there had been a teenager working for them by that description, but he had died last week. "We went looking for him and found him dead beside the Dumpster. No one had seen a thing!"

I apologized, explaining that I must've been mistaken. I didn't know the kid; he must have gone to a different school than I did. The stock boy had started to drift away, his lanky frame drooping with disappointment as he turned. That's when I noticed that his skin was glowing with a greenish cast, and the edges of his face seemed blurred even in the harsh supermarket lights. How had I missed that? "What was his name?"

"Henry Dawes."

"I'm sorry," I said, with an automatic politeness my mother would've been proud of. "I must've been mistaken."

The manager pointed to a poster in the window. It offered a reward for any information leading to an arrest for the murder. The manager changed the subject. "Are there any stains on your clothing? We'll be happy to take care of the dry-cleaning expense."

I waved him off. I kept watching Henry, as the manager offered me a coupon for ten dollars off my purchases for my trouble. I accepted that. Mr. Jameson wandered off to finish his own shopping, his good deed done for the day.

Henry smiled and waved for me to follow him. It was getting late, and I hadn't had picked up anything for supper yet, but I could give him ten minutes of my time. I just couldn't resist the unspoken plea on his pale-greenish face, but if he got me with that green slime I remembered from *Ghostbusters*, we were going to have some serious issues.

• • •

I followed Henry to the back of the store. We ducked into an aisle to avoid an employee coming out of the stock room pushing a cart of cereal boxes. Henry floated through the door, and I hoped he'd wait for me until the coast was clear so I could sneak through. It did say "Employees Only," after all.

I checked the round windows in the metal swinging door, then pushed it open. Henry was right there. I followed him through the stock room, worried that I was going to get caught.

Henry held up a hand, stopping me near the loading dock. I heard voices. They got louder as they got closer.

"You hear about that crazy girl that came in and said she saw Henry?" An angry male voice drifted over as I ducked behind a stack of boxes.

The second voice was also male, but younger, unsure. "I heard she claimed someone threw a grape at her head. That was Henry's favorite prank."

"Get it right, moron. It was a strawberry, not a grape."

"I don't care. It's still weird. Can you explain the shelf of toilet paper that fell over on its own last night? Or what about the tampon boxes falling on your head last Sunday?"

Henry winked at me and I couldn't help but grin back. He'd been having fun with his former co-workers. I was glad I'd stayed to see what was so important to him, but that didn't stop me from being worried. How would I explain being here if they caught me? Wait a minute. I was following a *ghost*. Maybe the simplest explanation was the most likely one: I really was losing my mind.

They stopped in front of the boxes I was hiding behind. I was conscious of how loud my heart was beating, and just breathing sounded like a beacon announcing my hiding place. Henry disappeared from view. I stayed behind the boxes, fear gelling in the pit of my empty stomach as they kept talking.

I couldn't see their faces. The box in front of me started to shift, and I thought I was going to throw up. Or get killed. Before I could decide which one would happen first, I heard a crash. Everything was silent for a heartbeat, and then the younger voice was laughing.

"Dude, you just got hit with an entire case of Massengill! I bet it's Henry calling you a douche, man. That's a riot!" He laughed.

I grinned as I saw Henry smiling, floating back over to my hidey hole. I could tell whatever he'd done had strained him; he looked less solid, and more green than he'd looked earlier. His skin was taking on the shade of the old green glass 7Up bottles my uncle collected in his garage. "Are you okay?" I mouthed at him.

He shrugged. Apparently he couldn't speak, but that wasn't a bad thing. Even if they couldn't hear him, I'd have a hard time not responding, and we weren't out of the woods yet. The laughter stopped at the sound of a pistol being cocked. "Hey, man," I heard. "That's not cool." I agreed.

"Neither are these stupid pranks. For all I know, you're rigging the boxes to fall on me. Do you really think that's smart? You wanna end up like that nosy Henry?"

"Hey, Damien, I wouldn't do that. He's the one who got in your face, not me. You take care of me. Why would I want to go mess that up?"

I assumed the gun got put away, because Damien's voice told the other boy to go store the "boy" while he took care of the "girl." My eyes widened as I stared at Henry; I hoped Damien didn't mean us. When Henry finally gave the all-clear, I stood up and saw two young men standing by the time clock. They headed out the door without looking back.

"What have you gotten me into?" I was ready to give up shopping at this Kroger's for the next millennium if I had to, just to avoid Damien.

Henry gestured toward the back door beside the loading dock.

"No. I'm done. You're going to get me killed."

His eyes shimmered. Could ghosts cry? He clasped two hands in front of his chin, begging, and mouthed one word. Please.

I'm such a sucker.

• • •

I insisted that Henry show me what the boys had stashed. He pointed to some lockers and spun the dial himself to open the combination locks. It took a lot of pantomime and reading his lips to figure out what most of this stuff was; I'd never seen illegal drugs before. Inside the locker was a plastic fishing tackle box that turned out to be a portable pharmacy. Inside, the drugs were sorted like lures in colorful piles. "Boy" was crack cocaine. "Girl" was heroin, a brown residue in small twists of paper and gel tabs. I saw needles and pipes and rolling papers, and a small baggie of marijuana on a shelf above my head.

Even to my inexpert eyes, it was a small fortune in feel-good substances. I didn't even know what half of this stuff was until Henry found a way to tell me. "Henry, were you dealing drugs?"

An emphatic shake of the head told me no.

"Did you catch them dealing drugs?"

A nod. Yes.

"Did they kill you for it?"

He nodded his head again, and I was on the verge of telling him that I didn't really want to join him. Green isn't my color. He pointed out his own locker and spun the dial to open it. There wasn't much inside, but on the floor of the locker was a worn, faded photograph of Henry, more solid and not green at all, hugging a young girl and an older woman who looked like him. I assumed it was his mom and his sister. I felt bad for them; maybe Henry needed my help to show them that he died doing the right thing. Despite how cheesy it sounded, I'd want the same thing.

"Okay, Henry, I'll follow you now." Besides, Damien and his buddy had a gun. I wouldn't be safe until I could turn it all over to the police. How hard would it be for Damien and his friend to figure out that I was the one who saw Henry? I didn't live all that far away from Kroger's. The manager had my name and phone number in the incident report. I'd have to help him, or I'd never feel safe.

I waited for him to give me another all-clear before I went back to the door he'd indicated earlier. As I waited, I realized that he was fading after his efforts with the combination locks. I wanted to ask if he was okay, but I was afraid gestures would tax him even more. What happened if he went too far before I learned his secrets? I didn't know, and was afraid to think about it.

I went outside, and he pointed me to a Dumpster behind the store. I really hoped he wasn't going to have me climb into the trash; I'd just gotten this sweater for my birthday last week.

Henry pointed at the bottom of the Dumpster and I got on my hands and knees to look underneath. I could feel the asphalt digging into my knees through my slacks and I saw faint red stains just inches from my knees. I looked up at Henry and he nodded. The stain marked where he'd died. I hoped he hadn't suffered long, all alone with the rotting vegetables.

When I opened my eyes, I saw Henry's hand, so pale I could see through it, reaching under the Dumpster. I extended my hand to reach after his and my fingers encountered a hard plastic object.

It was a cell phone. I tried to turn it on, but the battery was dead.

"Yours?" I asked, my voice barely a whisper.

He nodded.

I wondered what could be so important about his cell phone that he'd risked so much to show me. I started to ask, but he held his finger over his lips and pointed to the back of the Dumpster. It was a tight squeeze, but I got behind the Dumpster just in time to hide from an SUV pulling up to the back of the store.

The couple in the SUV sat for a minute, looking around like birds trying to avoid a predator. The driver, a young girl of about sixteen with braids in her hair, was talking on her cell phone. I couldn't make out the conversation for the music blasting through the car's speakers. She wasn't on the phone long.

I heard another voice approaching and recognized it as Damien. The music shut off and I heard them talking as Henry motioned for me to stay silent. He didn't have to ask twice.

"Hey man, you holding?" I heard the driver ask.

"I got some hard, how much do you need?" I recognized Damien's voice, confident and assured.

"A twenty, that's all I got."

I saw them exchange something through the window, but I couldn't tell what it was. From what I'd seen in Damien's locker, I figured that "hard" was another slang term for illegal drugs. Cheerleading camp certainly hadn't taught me anything about ordering drugs from a street dealer. Neither did the National Honor Society, or the Spanish Club. Was I that naïve? Apparently the answer to that question was yes.

Damien lit up a cigarette, and the harsh smell of burning tobacco helped clear some of the sickening food-rot smell from my nostrils. When the sale was complete, he left, his smoke trailing behind him like an evil tail.

I slipped out from behind the Dumpster, my heart in my throat. Henry drifted out from behind the trash and motioned for me to follow him, in the opposite direction that Damien had gone. I'd follow him anywhere as long as it took me away from Damien. I'd be happy to never see that kid again.

Henry went around the corner to the front of the store. I hoped he'd shown me everything; I was ready to go call the police and dump the whole mess in their lap before stopping for drive-through junk on the way home rather than going back inside for groceries. The peanut butter and jelly sandwich I'd had for lunch was a distant memory. I hoped Henry didn't have any more hiding in mind. My growling stomach would give us away.

I looked at my watch and was amazed to find I'd spent three hours following Henry around, playing charades to communicate and hiding from Damien. Night had fallen. My mother would be getting off work soon and would wonder why I wasn't home yet. Henry pointed to the reward poster on the front window that the manager had shown me earlier. He pointed at his cell phone, clutched in my right hand, and then he pointed to the detective's phone number printed on the poster. His phone was dead, so I rooted around in my purse for my own.

• • •

"Detective Rankin here."

"Are you still working on the Henry Dawes case? I've got some information for you."

I heard a loud crash and jumped, looking around for Damien and his gun before I realized the noise had come from the other side of the phone line.

"Sorry, I was asleep. I knocked over a lamp getting out of bed. Yes, I'm still working the Dawes case."

"I'm standing in front of the Kroger's where Henry worked, looking at the reward poster, holding Henry's cell phone in my hand. You might want to come get it; I don't really feel safe here." I kept looking around for anyone who might be watching me. Hearing Damien threaten his friend earlier had made me paranoid.

"What's your name, ma'am?"

"Julianna Kent. Look, I found the cell phone right near where Henry was killed, and I overheard an employee talking about Henry. His name's Damien and he's got drugs in his locker. I saw him sell some to somebody and he's got a gun and he's still hanging around…" My voice got higher and higher as I talked, cramming my words together to get them all out.

"Look, I know the Kroger's you're standing in front of. Give me the description of your car and the plate number, and go sit in your car with the engine running so you can get away if you see Damien. I'll stay on the line. It will only take me ten minutes to get there. Does this Damien know you heard him?"

I started toward my car, giving him the plate number and trying not to draw attention to myself by breaking into a run in a deserted parking lot. I heard a noise behind me and turned to look, panic making a sour taste in my throat.

"There she is. Stop her!"

I hung up and ran. It was Damien. My legs churned under me as I bolted away from the store. There weren't any other open stores in the shopping center other than the grocery store, and I wasn't going to turn around. That only left me with running toward busy Smithville Road hoping ten minutes would pass quickly and the detective would show up.

By the time I passed the ATM at the edge of the parking lot, I was gulping for air, my lungs burning from lack of oxygen. Henry was in front of me, gesturing wildly. If I'd had the air to speak, I might have told him to go to hell. Maybe it was a good thing I couldn't; would telling a ghost to go to hell be insensitive and rude?

Damien was getting closer. I could hear his footsteps getting louder even as I hugged the edge of the ATM and tried to catch my breath. I turned and looked around the corner, and the light from the street lamps reflected off of something metallic in Damien's right hand.

I heard a gunshot and felt the bullet whiz past me. I couldn't stay here. I had to try to get away, or at least hide Henry's cell phone where the detective would find it, away from Damien. I shoved it in the front waistband of my slacks and pulled my shirttail and sweater out to cover it. There really wasn't another place to stash it.

I took off, running for the street. I ran out into the first lane, looking over my shoulder as horns blared in my ears. Damien was too close for comfort, but he had to wait for several cars to pass before he could follow me, his friend from the stock room urging him to just leave it alone before they got in more trouble.

I could hear Damien's voice over the honks and screeching of tires as the traffic rushed by on their rush to the highway. "Man, we're both going down if she gets away. She knows something about Henry."

Another gunshot rang out as I was about to step off the median. I turned just in time to see Damien's friend crumple, screaming in pain. Damien started to cross the street after me. I stepped into the next lane.

He flew toward me and I wasn't looking at the traffic until I heard the horn.

A semi-truck was coming at me. I heard the whine of his air brakes and the roar of his horn and knew I couldn't get away. I was going to die, but at least it wouldn't be at Damien's hands. I screwed my eyes shut, bracing for the pain that would come when I was shoved from behind.

I lost my footing and flew through the air, landing on the shoulder of the road with a painful thump as my head hit the edge of the pavement. I looked up to see Damien screaming, his mind deserting him as Henry, solidly forest green with effort, held Damien firmly in front of the oncoming truck, awaiting a deadly impact. Damien was looking directly at Henry, and there was no doubt in my mind that the two boys were staring at each other in Damien's last moments.

The truck came to a stop forty feet past impact, and I heard a gun clattering uselessly to the ground, out of reach.

My head throbbed and my stomach rebelled, emptying itself onto the gravel shoulder. I rolled over and saw Henry floating, almost invisible, above me. I could barely see him; the green skin tone was gone as well. My hand reached down to check his phone. It was still there.

I could hear the sirens off in the distance, wailing and screaming as they got closer. My head pounded in time with their noisy symphony, and I nodded to Henry. "I've got it from here. I'll make sure the police see this, and that your family learns how brave you were. Thank you for saving my life."

He nodded at me, and I saw his lips mouth the words, "Thank you, Julianna." And then he faded away into nothingness.

"Henry?"

There was no answer. I tried to sit up, but the world spun and I collapsed back onto the ground. He was gone. He'd faded more with each physical effort, and I realized he'd sacrificed what was left of himself to save me and to uncover the truth about his death. I patted the cell phone in my waistband as my world went gray and I passed out.

•   •   •

"Miss Kent? Ma'am, I need you to wake up, now." I felt a gentle pat on my cheek and opened my eyes. A paramedic shined a bright light in my eyes. I groaned, raising one hand to hide from the light.

"I'm awake," I said. "Is Detective Rankin here?"

"Yes, ma'am. He's standing outside, but I need to make sure you're okay." She poked and prodded, taking my pulse and blood pressure, muttering to herself. "You're going to be fine. I don't think you have a concussion, just some bumps and bruises. How do you feel?"

I took stock. "I'm sore, and I have a headache. I threw up earlier."

"Do you feel sick to your stomach now?"

"No. I feel hungry. I went to the store to get something to make for dinner, and I still haven't eaten." My stomach growled right on cue.

She laughed. "That's actually a good sign. You shouldn't drive home tonight, and stay home from school tomorrow. You're going to be plenty sore in the morning."

The EMT opened the door on a middle-aged, slightly rumpled man in a sweatsuit. He showed me his badge. "Miss Kent, I'm Detective Rankin, and I'm sorry I couldn't get here any faster. How are you feeling?"

I reached for the waistband of my pants for Henry's phone, but it was gone.

"Don't worry, ma'am. I've got the phone, and I've turned it over to an evidence crew to see what they can make of it." He leaned on the open door of the ambulance. "Do you feel up to telling me what happened tonight?"

I told him about Henry's poster in the window, and going out back to see the spot where Henry died. I left out Henry's ghost. I wanted him to believe me, not think I was crazy.

I told him how I'd found the phone, and about overhearing Damien and his friend talking about Henry and how they'd admitted to killing him. I finished by telling him how Damien's friend tried to stop him from going after me until he'd been shot, and about Damien's close encounter with the truck.

Detective Rankin's cell phone went off just as I finished. When he hung up, he turned back to me. "It looks like that was Henry's cell phone. All the e-crew had to do was charge it. Henry'd been taking pictures of Damien and his buddy—whose name is Charlie, by the way—dealing drugs out of the store for months."

"How did they get away with it for so long?"

He frowned. "He threatened his co-workers. The manager told me today that Henry reported what was going on, but that they didn't have any proof besides Henry's say-so. No one else would corroborate what he said, and there wasn't any evidence. Store security was investigating, but they hadn't found anything. Now they've all come forward." He walked away and started dialing on his cell phone again.

Just as he walked away, an older, secondhand Buick pulled up in the parking lot beside the ambulance. The EMT turned red.

"Who is that?" I asked.

"It's Henry's mother. She's an old school friend of mine, and I just couldn't resist calling her when I heard Henry's murder was solved. She lives just down the road. I shouldn't have called her, but I couldn't help it. She's been devastated by her son's death."

The driver got out of the Buick and walked up to me. I could see Henry's intelligent eyes in her face, and recognized her from the photo in his old locker. It had to be his mother. I shook her hand.

"Thank you. It helps to know that he was trying to do the right thing. And his little sister will be glad to hear that he helped get Damien off the street. He's been terrorizing the neighborhood since they were young."

I smiled at her. Somehow I knew Henry would be happy with the outcome.

I called my mother to come pick me up. Henry's mother showed me pictures of Henry and his little sister while I waited. I was happy, for her sake, that she finally had some answers to what had happened to her son.

When my mother arrived, she hugged me tight. "Honey, are you okay?"

I assured her that I was fine. Ms. Dawes and her friend, the EMT, backed me up. I'm not a homebody, but all I could think about tonight was going home. I wanted to feel safe and secure at home, especially knowing that Damien was out of commission.

After some wrangling about whether or not I should drive, we locked my car up for the night in the parking lot. We would come get it in the morning. The EMT had recommended that I not drive home, even though I wanted to. When we finally drove away, Mom asked, "Do you need anything before we go home?"

I gave her a weak smile. "Dinner. All this started because I needed stuff for dinner. I'm starving." My stomach growled. We laughed. Mom offered to order pizza. Despite worrying about whether I'd still fit in my cheerleader uniform tomorrow, I accepted. She called ahead with her cell phone and we picked it up on the way home. There's nothing like comfort food and letting Mom take care of me. And even though it hurt to laugh, it felt good. It was life-affirming. *This is for you, Henry*, I thought, as I squeezed her hand and thanked her before finally heading home to fill my empty stomach.

Addie King has nine years experience as a prosecutor handling adult felonies, misdemeanors, juvenile delinquency cases, and appellate work. She holds a degree in criminal justice from Ohio Northern University and a law degree from the University of Dayton School of Law. She spends her spare time reading, writing fiction, and trying to wean herself from home improvement shows, cooking shows, and video games. During the day, she practices law in Urbana, Ohio.

Cherry Bomb
by Johanna Harness

It wasn't my idea to put on the stupid play, and it wasn't my fault that Cassie Kincaid (aka the "Cherry Bomb") wound up dead. I blame Mrs. Larry, the English teacher. She's the one who told us we could get extra credit and pass the course if we put on a play. I'm not good at English—mostly because I'm not into analyzing the works of dead guys. Updating the curriculum by adding a story about an orphan from Latin America doesn't really help me identify either, so I needed the extra credit.

I've spent my life in the middle of sugar beet fields, in a house with a big front entry with lots of linoleum. I know a lot about kickin' off boots before I hit that red chintzy carpet my mom tried to keep "nice," and about falling asleep halfway to my bed because I'm so damn tired. I've grown up with a lot of kids who live in the same dated houses with the same old ways. Now, I'm supposed to feel the curriculum is more diverse because it includes old dead guys from Europe and the American South and Those States—the ones up in the right hand corner that I don't bother to remember because they don't know who I am so why the hell should I care about them. Those. And now I get to feel included because I have Latin American authors in my text? Yeah. Right.

So Mrs. Larry—that's her real name, honest—decides that those of us failing her class should have another way to get through it, and she gives us this option to put on a play. So really, what happened to the Cherry Bomb is Mrs. Larry's fault and not mine. I would never have agreed to all the stuff that led to Cherry's death if it weren't for Mrs. Larry's moldy old authors. And that crap story from Latin America.

• • •

So, yeah, I'm Betz Rigby and I decided it was up to me to figure out what happened before someone broke down and called our inept local law enforcement. Our cops are good for school assemblies, but you take one gun safety course from Jim Waters and you start worrying about community safety as a whole. I figured when the cops showed up for Cherry's body, they would need an explanation wrapped up like a birthday present.

· · ·

It all started the day before Cherry died.

"Betsy Rigby," said Mrs. Larry, "you'll be the scribe." And I was thinking how much that sucked because being scribe means you only get credit for writing stuff down, and everyone knows that's not really what happens. Everyone else sits around talking about pimped-out trucks and the latest movie and Megan Rudder's attitude, and you're stuck there with the damn pen, trying to make shit up so you don't all fail. And for that you get called a scribe. It's more like you should be called a brain-weaver, or a magician, or a mastermind of fools.

So I was thinking about redesigning my mental business card, and I kind of missed her announcement of the other people in the group. Seriously? I'm waiting for someone to come up with a diagnosis for my short attention span. Ever since Chucky Ross got labeled with a learning disability, his life has been sweet. I could use a label.

"Betsy!"

I looked up, and Mrs. Larry pointed toward the door.

Whatever.

She handed me a paper on my way out. I thought I was going to the counselor's office again, but I was barely in the hallway when Luce Loughry put her arm through mine. Luce is probably my best friend outside of Dougie Squim. Luce is all kinds of beautiful, and her parents are not beet farmers. Her dad retired from the military and she's lived all over the world—very glamorous. She talks about castles and museums and art galleries, and while other kids are pointing and clicking with their digital cameras, she's there with a sketch pad, capturing all the details.

"This is going to be fantastic!" she whispered. When she bounced on her toes, I believed it for just a second.

Then Cherry Bomb swung in on Luce's other side. "Your enthusiasm bites my dog," she said.

What did that even mean?

Then Roger Barooska jumped in behind Cherry. "You can bite my dog," he told her, and she giggled like the two of them were witty as all hell.

Great. Morons. Scribe of morons. I should have just written it down and turned it in. I would have too, except for the fact that I kind of wanted to pass the class.

So that's how it started. We set up in the drama room, and Stacie Lamont edged past Cherry to get the spot at the end of the table. Stacie liked to be seen. It was kind of her thing. Blond curls, popping gum, lots of lipstick and goo on her lashes, skirts short enough to leave next to nothing to the imagination. Stacie had a corner on come-hither-now-stop. She hated Cherry.

"Let's do a play about this cheap-ass place," said Matthew. His family was *The* Wilson Family, as in the Wilson Family Pharmacies. His clothes were worth more than my car. I hated him. If he'd been murdered, I'd be the prime suspect. He lifted a curl from Stacie's eyes and she beamed at him. I thought I might vomit.

"Let's make it a murder," I said, picturing blood on Matthew's fancy loafers.

He glanced in my direction, not really looking at me—like he wondered where that voice came from—then he turned back to Stacie.

For the record, when I suggested a murder, I didn't mean it literally. Just so you know. I did suggest it, but I was talking about the play.

Dougie slipped in next to me. He didn't really need to do the extra credit. He was acing the class, so he must have volunteered for my benefit. Several times he'd tried to explain to me that I wasn't to blame for the classroom's cultural distancing issues. I wasn't sure what that meant, but I liked the part about not being blamed. If Dougie could get that cultural distancing thing validated as a learning disorder, I might add benefits to our friendship. He smiled at me just then, like he could read my thoughts, and I decided it was time to get things going.

With the play.

"Where's my pen?" I just had it. I lifted up the books around me and looked on the floor and then a hand reached over my shoulder.

"You can borrow mine." I turned toward the voice. Jillie Dodger. I'd almost forgotten she was in the class. The girl was like water. One minute you saw her, and the next you weren't sure if she'd ever been there.

I stared at the pen. Same style. Same chewed nubby places. "That is not your pen," I told her. "That's the pen I'm missing."

She shrugged. "It's not," she said, "but you can have it if you're going to go all possessive. I can find another."

She walked smoothly behind Matthew. One moment his Montblanc was on the table. The next it was gone. I never took my eyes off her, and I didn't see her take it. I'm just saying: it was there and then it was gone.

"I have an idea," said Matthew. "Why don't we make this a play about murder?"

I stared at him. He had to know he was repeating me. Had. To. Know.

Roger edged up behind Cherry and drew a finger across her neck. "Maybe someone kills the hottie," he said.

Cherry grabbed his finger and bent it backward until he begged for mercy.

I looked down at the paper, ready to check off requirements. "Setting?"

"Locker room," said Roger.

"Where's my pen?" asked Matthew.

Stacie tipped her head toward the rich kid. "I'd be so nervous performing in a locker room." Matthew gulped and quit looking for his pen.

Veronica Derby suddenly thumped down in a chair and threw both hands down on the table. Her black hair came from a bottle and she arched a pierced brow. "Anyone needs anything for their stage fright, they can come to me."

"Not the place," I told her.

She arched the opposite brow toward me. "I'm just saying."

Luce suddenly flipped open her sketchbook and leaned forward to get a better look. Veronica turned toward Luce for a just a moment, smirking as if for a photo and not a sketch, then she slouched back in her chair.

I tapped the page. "Is everyone here? Maybe we should start with characters and go from there."

Barney Magnuson grunted from the doorway. "I'm here," he said. "Put my name down, but I have to leave early." He tapped his watch. "I have an experiment that needs attention."

Groaning.

Muttering.

Barney always got special treatment for his dumb experiments. Mr. Daltry thought the kid was Boy Genius or something. I suspected Daltry had something to do with this extra credit option. Barney couldn't fail

English and still get into the university where he would cure cancer or create rocket boots or whatever. And I had seen Mrs. Larry and Mr. Daltry whispering behind their hands. They were up to something.

"No locker room," I said. "The play has to be performed here." I pointed. "On that little stage. I am not building props."

"You know," said Matthew, "seems to me the locker room setting would add a lot of work in the form of building props."

Both Cherry and Stacie nodded adoringly at him and I thought my head might explode. He seemed to feel the menacing presence he could not see. "Where's my pen?" he asked.

Dougie tapped the table with his pencil. "Any volunteers for death?"

Veronica leaned forward, placed fingertips on the table again. "What's in it for me?" she asked. She stared at Dougie until he looked away. Then she grinned. When she leaned back, her leather jacket was gone.

"Volunteers?" asked Dougie. "Involves stage makeup probably."

Cherry clucked her tongue. "I'd do that," she said. "I'm good with make-up." She glanced at Stacie. "Not like some people." She mimed applying makeup way beyond her lips, clucked her tongue again, and rolled her eyes.

Matthew didn't look up. He simply put an arm to the side in time to hold Stacie back. Like they'd rehearsed it. Whole thing felt like a play already.

Luce finished her sketch, placed it in the center of the table, and everyone leaned in to look. In the drawing, Veronica arched an eye at Cherry and the second girl's lips rounded into a suggestive circle.

Cherry lunged across the table. "I do not look like that!"

Luce grabbed the paper before Cherry could get it. She slipped it into her notebook. "I draws 'em likes I sees 'em."

"What about the counselor's office?" asked Barney.

We all turned to look at him.

He shrugged. "For a setting. It would be easy. Desk. Chair. Someone could wear his stupid hat." He shoved off the wall. "I'll be him. Write me in." Then he walked out.

Fine. I wrote it down:

Mr. Galbraith, counselor

Cassie Kinkaid, victim

"I can get his hat," said Jillie. Girl was wearing Veronica's jacket.
We all stared.

"You know, a hat like it," Jillie said. "Just like it."

"That's my coat!" yelled Veronica.

Jillie slipped it off and dropped it in Veronica's lap. "It's mine. Gram
gave it to me. But Vampira can have it if it makes her feel better."

Veronica lunged at her. Seemed like lunging had turned into our
group thing. Not much contact though. No brawling. Jillie swept across
the room before I realized she'd moved.

"So? You want the hat?" she asked. I shook my head no, but everyone
else said things like, "Hell yeah!" and "Why not?"

Even Dougie: "You can get it tonight. Let's spend one night ad-
libbing, do this thing tomorrow, and not waste any more time on it."

"A-greed," said Luce, her enthusiasm gone. "Mrs. Larry will drag this
out to the end of the year if we let her. Then we're stuck in here every
class till the end of the semester."

We blinked at each other and everyone nodded in quick agreement.

• • •

I couldn't get my crappy car to start, so I had to walk and I was late.
Then all the school doors were locked. I recognized my friends' junkers
in the lot—plus Matthew's vintage BMW—so I knew they had to be in
there. I ended up crawling in the art room window. Luce spent a lot of
time there and she'd shown me how she jiggled the window until the
latch popped. Easy. And it's not like our school had the budget for a
security system.

As I walked toward the drama room, I started seeing shadows darting
back and forth, and I wasn't freaked out, just annoyed, because I didn't
know there was a dead body or anything. And eventually someone
shoved Dougie in front of me and he stumbled, and then tried to look
all casual. "So, hey," he said. "Hey, *Betz*." He said my name too loudly.

I pushed him against a wall and walked by him into the drama room,
and everyone shifted their eyes to the ground. "Talk," I told them. No
one talked, so I did a mental roll call. "Where's the Cherry Bomb?"

"That's probably not respectful," said Luce, "what with her being dead and all."

"Departed," said Matthew. "I think Cassandra has departed."

I searched the room for a single sane-looking classmate, ultimately deciding they'd started the play without me. Fine. I was late and they'd cast me as Dumb Girl #1. I looked at Stacie and she seemed more vacuous than usual. Maybe I was Dumb Girl #2. Whatever.

"Where is she?" I asked.

"Counselor's office," mumbled Roger.

I took long steps toward the office, with everyone running behind me. At Galbraith's door, my eyes widened. Cherry sat at the desk, her skirt up even higher than usual, blood running down the side of her face, the to-be-thieved hat propped on her head.

"That's some good makeup," I said. "Get up, Cherry. You're freaking me out."

Veronica sidled up next to me and slipped me a little blue pill. "Let me know if you need two," she said. "It's on the house. Under the circumstances."

I shook the pill at the group. "What are you saying? Cherry! Not funny!"

"You should take the pill," said Luce. "I'm pretty sure they won't kill you. Stacie's had three."

I tipped my head at Stacie and she waved at me.

I tossed the pill across the room and it hit the garbage. "Nobody leaves this room," I said. It sounded all dramatic, but no one listened to me.

Veronica went to the trash.

"Afraid you'll leave incriminating evidence?" I asked. "She die of an overdose?"

Veronica rolled her eyes. "I don't believe in throwing away things of value. You didn't want it, all you had to do was hand it back."

Jillie glided to the desk and I stared at her smoothness, finally realizing she wore roller skates. And not just any skates—big retro things, the kind you might find in your grandparents' basement. The girl was weird. She lifted Cherry's hat, revealing a dent that didn't look so good. Jillie did a spin on the skates and covered Cherry's head again. "Where were you at the time of death?" Rollergirl asked me.

"Locked outside!" I told her. "Since none of my classmates bothered to leave the door open for me."

"The door was locked?" asked Roger. "It was open when I came in."

Stacie shrugged. "We've all been together since we found her."

"Since *I* found her, you mean." Jillie made another circle as she said it.

Still digging in the garbage, Veronica snapped. "No! No more circles. One more circle and I cut you off."

Jillie stilled. She quit breathing for a bit. "Well I'm clear," she whispered. "If I did it, I wouldn't have come back and told you all she was dead."

"Unless you wanted us to think you were clear," said Matthew. "Maybe you killed her and then came and told us you found her that way."

Jillie started to spin again and Veronica snapped her fingers. Jillie stopped, bit her lip, and pouted.

"Can we go somewhere else?" Stacie asked. "Somewhere without a corpse?"

"Not until someone explains *this* to me," said Veronica. With a flourish, she pulled a paper from the garbage.

I grabbed it from her, figuring I was the only one not under the influence of little blue pills. The list, in Mrs. Larry's handwriting, contained all our names. I handed it to Luce and she passed it down the line. When it came to Dougie, he lifted his hands, palms out, and shook his head. "Why are we putting fingerprints on all the evidence?" he asked. "We like jail?"

Roger panicked. "We have alibis! We all agreed, all of us but her anyway." He pointed at me. "If the rest of us stick to our story, we won't go to jail."

"Just me," I said. "Nice."

"Come on, Betz," said Dougie. "He didn't mean it that way."

"Why not?" asked Roger. "From where I'm sitting, it seems like she very well could have done it. I don't know that anyone locked her out. Door was wide open when I came in."

"So you say." said Dougie. "Last time I saw Cherry alive, you had your hands all over her."

"I thought we agreed to call her Cassandra," said Matthew.

"Well, clearly the crime was committed by a guy," said Stacie. "No girl would leave another girl like that."

"With her skirt pushed up?" I asked.

She shook her head. "Lipstick smeared." Then she stared at me. "I guess it could have been you, though. You're not really much of a girl."

I closed my eyes and counted, fighting an impulse to increase the body count. Or trash-dive for the lost pill.

Luce slid in next to me. "You missed the worst of it," she said. I blinked at her.

"Back to the drama room," I told them. As I walked away, I heard a rattly sound and turned to see Roger pushing the dead girl on the wheeled office chair. "Not her!" I screamed. "Not. Her."

Roger nodded quickly. "Oh. Okay."

"I'll catch up," said Veronica. She glared at me. "I'm still looking for my stuff."

Barney hesitated. "Maybe I should stay here to watch you search."

"Meaning what?" Veronica snapped.

He shook his head. "I don't like you. You don't like me. I don't know what you might slip into her pockets. I'm not leaving you alone with her."

Roger went back to the office chair and raised his eyes at Barney. "You want for me to wheel her again?"

The rest of us yelled "No!" and Veronica picked up the garbage. "I'll take it with me," she said.

We all stared. The carpeting under the can was singed. Veronica lifted the can high and the bottom was charred black. Unceremoniously, she dumped it upside down. Papers fluttered from the top and ash floated down from the bottom. Veronica dug fingers into the mess and pulled out the pill. She popped it in her mouth and wiped black residue on her pants. "Let's go," she said.

"Are we trying to go to jail?" asked Dougie. "Really?"

"We could bury her," said Roger. "She's an easy roll." He demonstrated the wheel action on the chair.

"That's what all the guys said," Stacie answered.

Matthew pursed his lips. "That was beneath you," he told her.

"Cassandra was a lovely girl."

Jillie glided up behind the rich kid. "You should know." She twirled despite Veronica's evil glare. "Was she blackmailing you? I watched her peel off some twenties at the mall last week. Or was it payment for services?"

Matthew put his nose in the air and sniffed. At least I was no longer alone in my invisibility. I kept walking to the drama room, and the others straggled in behind me.

"First things first," I said. "I'm not covering up a murder, and if you all try to hang me out to dry, I'll tell the cops I heard you synching up your alibis. Second? If one of you plans to kill me, just do it now. I don't want to worry about shadows in the hallway."

Roger snorted. "Yeah, like a killer's going to step forward and kill you in front of the rest of us."

"You have the mind of a killer?" I asked.

Suddenly defensive: "Nuhhh."

"Door was open when you came in?"

"Wide open. Like standing open," he answered.

"Did Cherry reject you? Is that why you killed her?"

"I didn't kill her and that girl never rejected anyone."

"What about Dougie's claim? You see her after school?"

"What of it?" he asked. He slumped against the wall and I wanted to shake him. Except I didn't want to get close enough to shake him. You know?

"Well," I asked, "Is it likely the cops are going to find your DNA on the victim?"

No longer slumping, he started pacing. "Oh geez oh crap oh godz!" He ran a hand through his hair. "They're going to inject me!" He shook Dougie's shoulders. "Dude, don't let them kill me! I was with you! You have to tell them!"

I raised my eyebrows at Dougie and he shrugged at me. "Yeah, okay. I saw them leaving the band room and Cherry was definitely alive."

"And you what? You hung out with the Pro-Magnum dude after they split up?"

"Cro-Magnon," said Dougie. "We shared space. It's not like we were hanging together. I was sitting against my locker and he was sitting against his. We were both there when Jillie started shrieking."

"So you two can truly alibi each other?" I asked.

"Yes!" yelled Roger.

"I'd feel better if it were someone else," said Dougie. "Someone whose physical evidence wouldn't tie me to the crime."

"So neither of you actually left the school?" I asked. "When you said the door was wide open, Roger, when was that?"

He ducked his head.

"During the school day?"

He nodded.

I knew where Dougie's locker was, but not Roger's. "Neither of you could see the office from where you were? The main doors?"

The both shook their heads.

I turned to Veronica next. "Did you leave after school?"

She shook her head. "I was here helping some kids cope with their stress."

"You weren't outside dispensing meds?" I asked. "Not at all?"

Her eyes widened. "Are you crazy? There are drug dealers out there. I don't do drugs. I have prescriptions. Reputable manufacturers and everything." She patted a pocket. "I can get you a prescription too, if that's what you need. It's all legit. I have Barney check for authenticity when I'm not sure."

We all turned to look at Barney. "Public service," he said.

The pressure in my head continued to build. I turned back to Veronica. "Was Cherry one of the kids you helped with stress?"

"Nah. I saw her, but she didn't want to relieve stress. She wanted some morning-after pharmaceuticals. I couldn't help her."

"Did you argue about it?" I asked.

"Nope. I sent her to Barney. He's been doing some custom compounds for Mr. Daltry and I thought maybe he could help her."

Barney hit a wall. "God, Veronica! We had a deal!"

"The two of you killed her together?" asked Luce. "But why?"

"Don't be so naïve," answered Stacie. "Cherry must have threatened to turn them in."

"No!" yelled Barney. "It's not like that. I'm helping Mr. Daltry with medical research. It's all legitimate."

Veronica nodded. "I'm helping Daltry too. I get a lot of your supplies for you." She nodded at Barney earnestly. "We're good people."

"What do you mean you get supplies for me?"

"The cold medicines and stuff," she answered.

Barney's eyes went wide.

"Dude!" yelled Roger. "Daltry has you cookin' meth!"

"No," said Barney. "He wouldn't do that. He's helping me with scholarships. He said he'd pay my tuition." He paused and his face turned red before he dropped into a chair. Head in hands, he moaned. "I'm not going to college, am I? I'm going to jail."

"So what did you say when she came to see you?" I asked. "Could you help her?"

"Uuuuhhhh," he said.

"Barney! Snap out of it. What did you tell her?"

"I wasn't there."

"What do you mean you weren't there? How do you know she came by if you weren't there?"

"Because she was still there when I came back."

"Well what did she say?"

Barney got up so abruptly his chair toppled over behind him. "She was dead, okay? She had a big dent in her forehead."

"You moved the body?" asked Veronica. "Really? Don't you know that makes you look guilty?"

Barney threw his hands in the air. "Of course I moved the body! You think I wanted them to find it in the middle of my experiments? I went and got Galbraith's chair and I rolled her into his office."

"How'd you get in?" asked Jillie.

"The door was open. I locked it behind me. How did you get in?"

"I'm good at locks," answered Jillie. "I went in to take the hat, and there she was. Why'd you put her there?"

"To throw suspicion on the rest of us," said Matthew. "He knew we were doing a play about murder. He knew Cherry had agreed to play victim. He knew we were using the counselor's office for our setting. Where are your notes, Betz?"

"Why?" I asked.

"We have to get rid of them. Don't you see? He's framing us for

Cherry's murder! We have to get rid of your notes or it will look like we planned this thing!"

"Don't have a coronary, Richie Rich. I left them here."

"Where?"

"I don't know. Here. We were coming back tonight. Why carry them around? I barely wrote anything."

We all searched but couldn't find the paper. Stacie interrupted us. She'd lost some of her pharmaceutical glaze and turned on Matthew. "I'd still like to know where Cherry got the cash. Drugs like the kind she wanted couldn't be cheap."

"Pharmaceuticals," said Veronica.

"Whatever," said Stacie. "I want an answer."

Matthew shrugged. "Fine. She said I was responsible. I doubt I was, but she was a fine girl and I gave her some pocket change."

"You weren't motivated to kill her?" I asked.

"I make my problems go away with money, not violence."

The room was silent for a beat.

"Despicable," said Jillie, "but he seems honest about it."

We nodded. We were losing our prime suspects pretty rapidly.

"What about Luce?" Matthew asked. "Cherry hated that drawing. Did she come after you? Maybe it was self-defense."

"Nope," said Luce. "And if she were looking for me, she'd have found me in the art room. I was there the whole time. What about you, Stacie? Jealous your boyfriend knocked up the Cherry Bomb?"

Stacie didn't answer. She ground her teeth together and stared daggers through Matthew.

"I think it's safe to assume she just found out," I said. "If Matthew turns up dead, we'll have at least one suspect."

"What about Mr. Daltry?" asked Jillie. "If he found Cherry snooping around in his lab, he might have taken her out."

"Not his style," said Barney. "He'd have found out what she wanted most and given it to her. It's what he does. That's how it worked with Mrs. Larry. Her husband is sick and they couldn't afford the experimental drugs."

"Gah!" Jillie hit her forehead. "That's why we're doing this stupid play?"

"Yep."

"Why were our names on that paper?" asked Veronica.

Matthew shrugged. "We were being offered a deal. Things like that go through the counselor."

"And how would you know that?" asked Luce.

"My parents are great sponsors of school events," he answered. "You think they do it out of civic pride?"

"It doesn't matter," said Dougie. "The list was insignificant or it would have been burned."

"What's up with that anyway?" asked Jillie. "Who burns stuff in a garbage can?"

"People who go to a school with no smoke detectors," answered Luce. "Maybe if Matthew fails another class, we can get some."

A picture of the lost paper flashed through my mind. "Oh crap. I think I've got it. We have to go back there."

Stacie's eyes widened and Veronica put an arm around her. "It's okay," she said. "I have something to calm your nerves."

Jillie made it to the office first. When she opened the door, we all gasped. Cherry was gone. The trash was gone. The office looked disturbingly normal.

"We have to get out of here," I told them. "The killer's still here. He came back to his office."

"Mr. Galbraith?" asked Luce.

I nodded. "I only wrote two things on that paper: Mr. Galbraith, counselor and Cassie Kinkaid, victim."

The sound of a shotgun cocking sent a jolt through us. We jerked around and there was Galbraith, leaning against his doorframe, wearing his hat.

"You left the note in full view," he said. "I went to discuss your little extracurricular arrangement with Mrs. Larry and there was the note. I came back here, burned it, and then I saw Cherry in the hallway, so I followed her."

Seemed to me he was in another world as he talked.

"I only planned to confront her, find out what she was telling everyone. But when I caught up with her she was confiding in Veronica about her pregnancy—conspiring to kill my child without even telling me it existed. She had no right."

The guy was freaking me out. I was so chilled I needed a parka, but he continued:

"I caught up with her in the science lab. When I confronted her, she lunged at me, said I could bite her dog—whatever that means. When I pushed her back, it was self-defense, I swear to God it was. But obviously no one would see it that way. So I went for a walk, to get my thoughts together. When I came back, I found my office door closed…locked. Cherry was here and my garbage turned over and I knew you all were trying to mess with my head, get me to go crazy. I have a degree in psychology. I'm not stupid."

He eyed us all. "And that's when I realized how unstable Roger Barooska is…how he assaulted Cherry and then turned a shotgun on your innocent little drama group. I would have died too if I hadn't wrestled the gun away from him and shot him in the process. Schools are such dangerous places these days."

Galbraith lifted the gun and I cringed, preparing to die. Then his eyes went huge. I mean really huge. He dropped the gun and fell forward. A Montblanc pen was sticking out of the back of his neck.

"It's my pen," said Jillie. "My Gram gave it to me. But he can have it. He seems pretty attached to it."

• • •

Thankfully, local law enforcement accepted our story after it was sanitized by Mr. Daltry. Barney no longer needed to work in the lab and was given a full-ride scholarship to an impressive private school. Veronica quit her side job too, and she's planning to become a pharmacist. Stacie's working with a real doctor and getting some legal prescription meds. Jillie changed schools—just vanished like she was never there. And, of course, we're all once again invisible to Matthew. Luce wrote a graphic novel about our experience, Dougie is still holding out for a friendship with benefits, and Mr. Daltry says there's a scholarship waiting for me alongside Barney's. Oh—and Mrs. Larry's husband made a full recovery. He's going to be our new schoolcounselor. His name is Larry. Larry Larry. That's his real name. I'm going to talk to him about diversifying our curriculum. The one story about the Latin American kid just doesn't cut it. We need at least a few authors who understand the charm of rural life.

Johanna Harness taught college English for ten years before beginning the adventure of homeschooling her own children. She writes middle-grade and young adult novels in both northwest and fantastic settings (often forgetting which is which). She is the creator of the Twitter hashtag #amwriting and can be found posting there in her early morning hours.

Toothless
by J.A. Souders

The sound of her heart racing urges me forward.

She is mine.

From the minute our eyes met across the dance floor of Hades—New York's oldest eighteen-and-under club—I knew it. And I hadn't wasted a single moment to get her alone and in my arms.

Even when she realized what I was and tried to sneak away, I knew. And now, with her feet slapping the wet concrete of the alley, her heart hammering in her chest, and her breath gasping, her blood beckons to me. Like a Siren's song, it is impossible to ignore.

The red-haired beauty has wound her way around the city, dodging here and there, but I'm never far behind. And while I'm not hurrying, to her mortal eyes, I am a blur.

Taking her before this started would have been easy, but the chase is fun. In a life filled with endless night, a little entertainment with my meals is indispensable and key to preventing boredom—a fate worse than a stake through the heart. At least there's a fight before the stake.

But the chase has come to an abrupt end. Poor thing. She's run right into a dead-end alley. An apt name…considering.

"Please," she begs, her whole body shaking with the fear that pours off her in large, succulent waves. "Please don't hurt me."

"Oh, this won't hurt in the least," I say. However, the fangs gleaming from my smile probably don't offer her much relief.

She pushes herself against the wet, dirty wall as if trying to go through it, and I have to laugh. Why do mortals always think that cringing away from a monster is going to make us go away? Seriously. Damned mental, if you ask me.

"Relax," I say. "This really won't hurt. You'll never feel a thing."

As I step closer, the fear radiating from her causes me to quiver in anticipation. Her blood will be delicious. Like the first taste of a fresh, tart, not-quite-ripe apple.

Toe-to-toe with the girl now, I place my hands on either side of her face. Her brown eyes are wide and barely visible because the black depths of her pupils have taken over.

Her lips, painted a bloody red, tremble, but it's not all fear now. It's just as much arousal. Anticipation.

It's such a shame really. She is a beautiful girl. I trail my finger down her delicate throat and rest it in the hollow of her collarbone. Maybe I'll keep her after all. She would make a wonderful companion.

She's making little whimpering sounds that make me want to moan with pleasure. *Is there anything more electrifying than a moan?*

I smile, then dip my head, brushing her lips with mine, letting her breathe in my scent, which is more potent than any illicit drug. Almost immediately it takes effect and she's putty in my arms. If I weren't pressing my body firmly against hers, she would fall to the ground.

I shake my head. Humans really are strange creatures. But this makes it easier for me as I shrug and lean over her. My breath flutters her hair as my fangs lengthen. Then I press them against her skin, expecting to feel a small resistance, then a pop and the salty-rusty flavor of her blood filling my mouth.

Nothing happens. They can't penetrate.

What the hell? Maybe I just didn't press hard enough. Sometimes if humans do a lot of indoor tanning, it makes the skin leathery, so I push harder. Nothing.

With a frown, I pull back to look at her skin.

Still nothing. Not even a mark or an indent. How strange.

I touch her skin with the tips of my fingers. Soft and supple. *So why am I having trouble?*

I try again. No matter how lovely her skin is, I'm going to pierce it. I'm not giving up. All her strange resistance did was make me want it more.

Using as much force as I can, I squeeze my mouth shut.

Snap!

A sharp pain fills my mouth, as does blood, but it's my own, not the girl's.

Holding my hand under my chin, I yank my mouth away from her throat. Not just one, but *both* of my fangs fall into it.

With a growl, I ball my fist and punch the chain link fence beside her head. I narrow my eyes at her. "What are you?" I ask, even though I know she can't answer. She's still out cold.

Snarling, I flip her over my shoulder and bound out of the alley, cursing her and my dumb luck to have found her in the first place.

• • •

I plop her unceremoniously on my bed, then debate whether or not to secure her to it, but she's not going anywhere. Even if she runs, I'll be able to bring her back.

My mouth is still bleeding and it aches like a you-know-what. I'll need to take care of that before I do anything else.

With a quick swish of my hand, I charm the door to the rest of the apartment, making it impossible for her to open. Then I step into my bathroom to rinse out my mouth. When I spit into the sink, my stomach growls, reminding me I haven't eaten yet.

I glare out at the girl. *What is she?* I've never had a problem with any other human before, which makes me think she's something more than a human. *But what?*

Pushing cotton balls into the empty spaces where my fangs used to be, I watch her.

She's still out. And I'm not quite sure what to do about it. No one has ever passed out on me *before* I drank from them.

Maybe I used too much Influence.

Well, too late now. Nothing to do but wait for her to wake up on her own. I won't be able wake her up. Not with Influence spiraling through her veins like anesthesia.

I debate whether or not to open a window and let some cool air blow across her face, in the hopes of flushing out some of it. But I don't want her to try and escape before I can get answers.

Wading through the piles of dirty clothes, empty junk food wrappers, bags, and empty soda bottles, I cross to the other side of the room to make sure the window is secure. Some runaway cheese doodles crush under my feet and I wince.

Mom is going to stake me if I don't clean this up. Especially when she finds out I brought a girl home. Double especially when she realizes *why* I brought this girl home.

But I'm still hungry. Well, I'm just going to have to fix that. With fangs. Or without.

Trying to think of a solution, I go back to the door and twist the handle, still walking. Considering it's still charmed it's no surprise when I smack right into it, jarring my already aching mouth.

I rub my nose. *Damn, that hurt!* With a growl and a wave of my hand I lift the charm on the door. *Stupid charm. Stupid Influence. Stupid girl.*

Vlad, my dog, is snoring on the woven rug in the center of the room. He doesn't even lift an eyelid as I stomp past and shove through the swinging door into the kitchen.

The white surface of the counters gleams at me, mocking me about the state of my room and my predicament, but I ignore it and go straight for the utensils drawer. It takes me about five minutes before I pull a carving fork from the drawer and stare at it.

This is perfect. With a smile, I grip it tightly and go back into the bedroom.

The girl is still out. Well, that's a bonus. I can't imagine she'd like it too much if she saw me coming toward her with a huge two-tined fork. Then again, she deserves it. Breaking my teeth like that!

Just in case she wakes up when I stab her, I charm the door again. Then I grimace. This is going to be messy. *I should do this in the kitchen for easy clean -up!*

Gripping the fork in my mouth, I drag her up and over my shoulder again. This time I remember to uncharm the door, and carry her into the kitchen.

She slumps in the chair, so I tilt her head back to get to her neck more easily. I remove the fork from my mouth and clutch it tightly in my hand. Raising it above my head, my eyes focus on the spot on the neck I want. The best place is the jugular, and even though I can stop the blood with a few drops of my own, it will spray everywhere. I'll have to be quick.

Before I can shove the fork into her throat, I remember I'm wearing my favorite t-shirt. I strip it off, then my jeans, so I'm just in my boxers. I probably look like an idiot, but I won't have to explain to my mom why my favorite clothes are gone.

Then I stare at her. I'll have to cover her clothes. There's no way I'll be able to take her back home if she's covered in blood. That's all I need—some wannabe knight in shining armor calling the cops.

I grab the box of trash bags under the sink and tear a hole in one of them, pulling it down over her shoulders. It covers her from neck to waist. Then I place another across her legs and another on the floor for good measure.

My stomach growls. "Yeah, yeah. I know. I know. I'm working on it," I grumble. Then I take a firm grip on the fork again and raise it above my head. Rolling onto my toes, I lean forward a little, making sure I move quickly.

With a grunt, I ram the fork down.

To my surprise, it just bounces off!

I glance at the fork. The tines are blunted on the ends.

Disgusted, I toss the fork down and go back to the drawer to root around. I find a crab fork and test the ends. Black blood wells when the two prongs break my skin. "Yep, you're sharp enough."

I step back over to the girl. "All right, beautiful. Let's try this again."

Once more I get into my stance. And roll up onto my toes. The crab fork above my head this time. I bring it down and…nothing. Again!

I study the fork and see it's blunted, too. I glare at the girl.

"What are you?" I demand, then toss the crab fork at the wall. It makes a *thwong* sound and wiggles when it sticks.

"So it was sharp enough to pierce the wall, but not your skin?" I narrow my eyes. "Interesting."

I go back to the counter. This time I attack the knife block, pulling them all out. One of them is going to work. It *has* to. No one's skin is thick enough to block all of our knives…

• • •

An hour later I stand huffing and puffing in the kitchen, the latest of my piercing equipment slammed into the wall across from me, joining all the others. Knives, forks, scissors, knitting needles, even an ice pick.

The girl is still out cold. Nothing I've done has stemmed the hunger pains in my belly. All I've accomplished is to poke holes in Mom's kitchen wall and work myself into what she calls a tizzy.

I can't believe this girl's skin is so resistant! She isn't human. That much is obvious. The question is, what is she? And why can't I pierce her damn skin? I'm hungry!

Then it hits me. Dad's sword! It's in the den, hanging on the wall.

Supposedly a gift from King Arthur after Guinevere's betrayal.

I run to the room and pull the sword from the wall, laughing as little rivulets of sweat run down my face and blood pools in my mouth. My heart beats faster. Yes, I do have a heartbeat, contrary to popular opinion. All vampires do. It's just too slow for humans to hear.

In the mirror behind the sword stand, I catch a glimpse of myself. My eyes are wild, and my hair is standing on end.

I fear I may be going mad from trying to get this thing to bleed, because as much as I want to eat, I want to watch this one bleed more. It's no longer just about eating, but it has everything to do with proving myself. Yes, I'm aware it's completely pointless and stupid. But at this point, I don't care. It's my manhood hanging on the line.

The sword is a bit heavy, which is perfect. The heavier it is, the easier it will cut through the flesh. That's been my problem. I've been using small, easy to wield things. It looks like the answer is going to be heavier, sharper things.

I grin as I walk over to the girl. "I'd like to see you escape this!" I say.

Hefting the sword over my shoulder, I rush toward the girl, and stop abruptly when I see she's woken up. Her brown eyes stare into mine. She smiles at me, just a tiny lifting of the corners of her lips.

"Well, well. Still haven't given up? I thought you had," she says in a husky voice with a Southern accent.

She licks her lips and stands. "I was starting to get disappointed when you were gone so long." She steps close to me, her fingers trailing over my arms.

"You were?" I ask, then shake my head. That is not the question I meant to ask. "I mean, how? You were under the Influence."

She chuckles, sending tingles of lust circling through my body. "No, I wasn't." She walks her fingers across my chest. "I was merely trying to figure out what you were." She tears the plastic bag from her shirt. "You were willing to kill me," she says with a pout. "That wasn't very nice."

I shake my head and swallow the ball of fear—and lust—forming in my throat. There's something wrong with this girl. She can't be a vampire, her skin is too soft and warm. But her eyes are turning red. "No, I swear. I was just going to take a little blood. Just enough to sate my hunger."

"Oh, then what's this?" she asks, running her finger along the blade of the sword.

I stare at it, not sure what I'd been planning to do actually. "I-I don't know."

She narrows her eyes at me and I feel a pressure in my head. She stares for the longest time, until she turns her eyes to the sword and studies it. She takes it from my hands and holds it as easily as Father does.

After a few minutes, she sighs. "What a pity. I had so been looking forward to a fight. But it seems you are under divine protection. Very well."

"If you were looking for a fight, why did you run away? You were scared. I could smell it!"

She laughs. "Just a little…entertainment before my meal."

She places the sword on the table, then grins at me. Two of her teeth lengthen to form two sharp points.

Oh, God. She's got fangs! I try running away, but it's as if my feet are glued to the ground. I can't move them. This must be how it feels when I chase my prey. If I live through this, I promise myself, I'll never play with my food again!

"What are you?" I gasp out.

"Me? I'm a *Krusnik*. A black angel." She shimmies her shoulders and large black wings unfold from her back, nearly touching the ceiling.

"Oh, God!" I say. It's not possible. No way. *Krusniks* are a myth. Killers of demons. Vampire drinkers. They don't exist.

But how can I deny it when one is standing in front of me? The legends were wrong about one thing—they aren't ugly, these bringers of death. She is beautiful. More beautiful now than when I thought she was human.

She steps toward me and brushes a hand over my hair. I try to push away, only to ram my back into the counter.

She laughs. "Why do vampires always think that cringing away from a monster is going to make us go away? Seriously. Damned mental, if you ask me. Logic fails!" Her smile grows wider. "This won't hurt. You may even enjoy it."

Oh, God. She heard everything I was thinking. And saying. She is *a Krusnik.*

She tilts my head to the side and, with only the slightest pain in my neck, begins suckling. A haze fills my head, as if I haven't slept in a few days. After a few seconds, I wobble and she helps me sit on the floor. It isn't long after that she disconnects herself. There's another pinch in my neck, then she helps me lean back against the cabinet.

"Thanks for the snack," she says with a smile, wiping the corners of her mouth. "I knew you'd be tasty."

She places the sword in my lap with my hands on the hilt, then looks into my eyes. "Stay away from Hades. Good boys like you should know better than to mess with the girls from there."

Unable to respond, I watch as she stands, folds her wings into her back, and leaves through the swinging door.

My eyes flutter closed as her words circle in my head.

Damn straight, I think, slipping into unconsciousness. *I'm never setting foot in that place again.*

• • •

When I wake, I'm still in the kitchen, but Mom and Dad are standing in front of me. Mom is shaking me and Dad is staring at the knives in the wall.

"Vance. Vance! Wake up, honey! What happened? Are you hurt?" Mom demands.

My head still swimming, I say, "No. I think I'm fine."

"What happened, son?" Dad asks, turning to face me.

Slowly I tell them. From me going to the club to eat, to ending up the floor in the arms of a *Krusnik*.

Mom watches me through the whole story and then snorts. "Red hair, you say?"

She picks up a black feather that's lying on the sword. "Well, that explains this." Then she stands up and gestures for Dad to help me. "How many times have I told you not to mess with redheads? They always come back to bite you."

J.A. Souders first began writing at the age of thirteen, when she moved to Florida and not only befriended the monsters under the bed, but created worlds for them to play in together. She is represented by the fabulous Natalie Fischer of the Sandra Dijkstra Agency, and blogs at Angels and Demons and Portals, Oh My! (jasouders.blogspot.com).

The Sea of Trees
by Kirsty Logan

I'm in the middle of the Shibuya crossing, surrounded by crowds of people ten-deep on either side, when I see my sister. Just one face among hundreds of others, but I know it's her. The shape of her nose, the angle of her eyebrows—it's just like mine.

"Cara!" I shout across the heads of the crowd. "Cara, wait! It's me!"

My words are muffled by the grumble of cars and the music pumping out of a dozen shop doorways. Everyone keeps their heads down and their feet moving; Japanese people do not shout in the streets, so everyone politely ignores me. The girl doesn't turn, but I can tell by the way she holds her shoulders that it isn't Cara.

I steer my feet past the escalators and the temples, the moon-high hotels and clusters of people at every crossing, wishing I could swallow my words back down. My parents might have given up looking for Cara, but I'll never stop.

I stand on the escalator leading into the Starbucks, my eyes blurring as I scan the endless crowds of people outside the glass walls. I can't see Cara—or rather, the girl who had looked like her—and I know it wasn't her anyway.

The girl behind the counter has hair bleached white with forest-green tips, and she wears a skirt that sticks out all around like a toadstool. At twenty, she's a few years older than me, but her high cheeks and pointed chin make her look like a schoolgirl.

"Hi, Mei!" I say.

"Hey, Cara!"

I met Mei nearly two months ago, and when she asked me my name the lie just slipped out. Now it's too late to tell her that my name isn't really Cara.

"Hazelnut mocha, please."

"Coming right up!"

Mei's accent is pure American Midwest; like me, she's third-generation Japanese. My features mean I blend into the crowd, but I'm London-born and only speak English even after six months in Tokyo. Over hazelnut mochas, Mei taught me *konnichiwa*, *domo arigato*, and *sumimasen* (hello, thank you, and sorry), and I use that last one most, as I haven't mastered the art of not bumping into people on the chopstick-thin streets.

I lounge at the counter, watching Mei while pretending not to. She slides my cup over, leaning in to add a final dusting of chocolate powder, and then grins at me.

"Have a great day!"

"Thanks."

I carry my mocha over to my usual seat by the window. I haven't even taken a sip when I sense that someone is behind me. Mei is holding a cloth as if she's meant to be wiping down tables, but really she's just standing next to my chair. Since the moment I met her, I've felt that there's something about Mei's face that makes me want to stare at her. Something familiar. Something about the shape of her mouth, the line of her chin…

"Sorry, had to wait for my boss to stop watching."

Mei glances around again, then throws her cloth onto the table. She slips into the chair next to mine and takes a big gulp of my mocha. I see her cheeks puff out before she swallows, and there's a dot of cream on her nose. She wipes it off on the back of her hand, then licks it.

"So, you want to go to Aokigahara?" She says it like it's a joke, but I don't get it.

I get out my phone. "How do you spell that?" As Mei spells the word, I thumb-type *Aokigahara* into Google maps, then tap the "train" button to see how to get there. "It's like three hours away. And there aren't any trains."

"It's an adventure. It's like a…like a pilgrimage. They're not meant to be easy. That's the point."

"But what is it?"

"They call it the Sea of Trees," she says.

"Okay…" I snort out a laugh. "So it's a forest? Big whoop."

"Oh, it's not just a forest."

I try to dig for more, but Mei just smiles in this annoyingly mysterious way.

Finally I accept that there's a point in going—though I still don't know what that point is—and ask how we'd get there.

Mei shrugs. "My boyfriend will drive us."

I don't know whether I'm jealous of Mei's boyfriend for getting to go out with her, or of her for having someone to go out with.

"Your boyfriend will drive you out to some weird forest in the bum-end of nowhere with some girl you barely know?"

"What? I totally know you. You've been coming here for months."

"Look, Mei, making someone coffee isn't the same as knowing them."

"Well, whatever. I still want you to come. It's an adventure."

"You said that already."

She starts untying her green canvas apron. "Well, I said it again because it's true. Now are you coming, or what?"

For a moment, I really do think about it. Running off on an adventure to some mystical wood with near-strangers. Finding another place to search, another chunk of land that might have the right answers. Another set of faces to check.

"I can't," I say. "I haven't finished my coffee."

Mei shrugs and drops her apron on the counter. Another girl is just stepping off the escalator, and she picks up Mei's apron, puts it on, and starts steaming some milk. I keep my eyes on the traffic outside until I'm sure that Mei has gone. When I take a sip of my mocha, it's lukewarm and the cream has curdled. I spit it back out and push the cup away.

Back outside the Starbucks a diamond of schoolgirls, all pleats and bunches, giggle at me. The girls here always giggle at me because they think I'm a boy. Tokyo women are dolls: petite and preened, thin as magazine models in their knee-skirts and bow-peppered blouses. Back home in England I'm a girlie-girl in my skinny jeans and pixie crop, but not here. My ex-pat school doesn't require uniforms, so they probably think I'm older than them. Older than them, and a boy. I keep my head down until I get on the train.

• • •

The next week of school passes in a blur of multiple-choice quizzes, lunches eaten while hunched over a book, and scratching out *kanji* figures with painful clumsiness. It might have been helpful for my parents to send me to Japanese classes before we moved here, but I think they're still mad that I didn't choose to go to the classes when I was younger. They barely speak it either, but lately they're all into the idea of heritage.

I'm a Londoner, born and bred. How the hell was I to know I'd need to speak the language of a country six thousand miles away?

Every evening, my Mum tries for hours to make *tan-tan-men*, then she gives up and serves us toasted cheese sandwiches. My Dad works until dark, then falls asleep on the train and misses his stop. No one wakes him up because half the other men on the train are asleep too.

One night, over plates of ready-made noodles, I try to mention Cara.

"Mum," I say.

"Hmm?" Mum is peering at a recipe book propped up against her glass. It's in Japanese, so I know she can't read it very well.

"Do you want to go by the university again this weekend?"

"What's that, love?"

I grab her book, slam it shut, and put it under the table. Mum looks at me with her eyebrows raised.

"The university, Mum. We could go and see if there's anything new there."

"Now, why would there be anything new at the university? Are you thinking of applying? You've got a few more years of school left yet."

"No, I mean that we could check the rooms, ask around to see if anyone's heard from…"

My voice trails off when I feel the heat of my Dad's glare. I'd thought he was dozing in his dinner, but now he's staring at me like I've just let out a string of curse words.

"Never mind," I say, and fill my mouth with noodles.

We weren't always like this, so strained and distant. Back in London I was close to my mum. We'd go out for milkshakes or to the cinema, then get on Skype and talk to Cara for hours. But nothing has been the same since Cara disappeared. We came all this way to find her, and then it's like they just forgot.

• • •

I go to the Starbucks in Shibuya every single day after school. I try to time it so I get there at the end of Mei's shift. We talk about American music and English actors and the foods we miss from home.

The months stretch, and no matter how hard I try I can't forget about Aokigahara. One morning school finishes early, so I go straight to the Starbucks. On the way, I phone my parents' house and tell them that I'm going to a study group, though I don't really know why because there's no reason to think I'll be home late. Just in case, I guess. My mum just mumbles Okay—she has been trying to make *gyoza*, but the dumplings keep coming out all gooey and uncooked in the middle.

At the top of the escalator, I see that Mei still has bleach-white hair, but now the tips are red. Her dress is covered in rows of black fringing, and every time she moves it looks like she's shimmying. When she sees me coming up the escalator, her face splits into a grin.

" 'Ello, 'ello," she says in a terrible English accent.

"What?" I know what she's doing, but I pretend I don't.

"I'm one o' yer English bobbies, guvnor. A proper copper. At your seeervice."

"Let's just stick to the mochas," I say, though I can't help smiling.

She makes up two mochas, then carries them over to my usual table and motions for me to sit down.

"Don't you have to, you know, work? It looks pretty busy."

Mei shrugs. "Kimiko will cover me. My shift's finishing in ten minutes anyway. I had classes this morning and I'm *tired*." She stretches out that last word into a yawn, covering her mouth with her hand.

I wrap my hands around my cup and decide it's now or never.

"What's the deal with Aokigahara anyway?" I ask. "Why do you want to go there?"

"It's the Sea of Trees."

"So?"

Mei won't say any more, just smiles at me and raises her eyebrow. I don't tell her, but I've already looked up Aokigahara on Wikipedia. It is called the sea of trees, but it's also called the forest of suicides. People say that if you wander far enough, you'll stumble on the bodies of people hanging from the branches or half buried under blood-stained leaves. The forest is so dense that there's no wind, and hardly any wildlife lives there. It's eerily silent and always dark. It's full of ghosts, so it makes sense that people who are looking for ghosts would go there.

"Can we get these coffees to go?" I say.

• • •

Mei's boyfriend is called Hayati, and I'm sure I'm saying it wrong because it keeps coming out of my mouth like Haiti, the country. The first few times, he corrected me, speaking so fast that I couldn't get my tongue around what he was saying. After that, he stopped bothering.

He and Mei are carrying on a fast-paced conversation in Japanese. I can't tell if it's an argument or not, and I gave up trying to understand about an hour ago. His car is tiny, even tinier than the cars back in England, but it's very shiny. Hayati must polish the red paint every day. I pretend to sleep, leaning back against the headrest and trying to picture Cara's face.

I must have dozed off for real, because suddenly Cara is there beside me in the car, the real Cara, just like when I last saw her two years ago. She's wearing a white dress and staring out of the window with her face turned away from me. *Cara*, I try to say, but no sound comes out of my mouth. I try to reach over and touch her shoulder, but my arms won't move. Cara lifts her hand and presses it against the window, and I see that outside it's night, and the trees are moving past the window far too fast, like the car has been strapped to a rocket. She moves her hand on the glass and I realize she's pointing at something, but everything is moving so fast outside that I can't see what she's pointing at, my eyes won't focus, and I realize that Cara's dress isn't white after all, and she's turning her head toward me. I'm scared to look but I can't look away and then she—

My head thunks against the window and suddenly I'm wide awake in the backseat. The back of Mei's head is right in my line of vision, and as she turns to look at Hayati I feel a jolt of recognition in my belly. The thread slips away, and I'm lost again.

I know without looking out of the window that we're on the outskirts of the woods. The silence is so absolute that it hurts my ears. I still haven't quite blinked the image of Cara out of my eyes, but Mei is up and out of the car, tapping on my window and motioning for me to follow her. Hayati leans back in his seat, tapping his fingers on the steering wheel.

"Aren't you coming?" I ask Hayati. He shrugs and picks at his fingernails. It takes a while for me to realize he's not going to reply. "Is that a yes or a no?"

"He won't answer you," calls Mei through the car window.

"He can't speak English?" It hurts my throat to shout, so I get out of the car.

"Sure he can. He just doesn't."

"What? That's so stupid."

"Oh yeah? How's your Japanese?" I'm looking off into the woods, but I can feel the intensity of Mei's stare. I'm here now, I suppose, and I might as well do this properly. I start walking toward the trees.

"Are you coming or what?"

. . .

As soon as we enter the canopy of trees, every sound is swallowed up. I never realized how accustomed I was to the noise of the wind in my ears until it was gone. All around us, shreds of orange plastic tape hang from the trees. Some of it still marks routes between the trunks, but most has been broken and lies tangled on the ground. Mei walks slowly, gazing all around her, even vertically up to the ceiling of leaves.

"So you never asked me." Mei speaks like she's talking to herself, and it takes me a while to realize I'm supposed to answer.

"Never asked you what?"

"Never asked me why I was here. In Tokyo."

I'm not sure whether we're still playing, but I try to force a smile. "Okay, so why are you here?"

Mei shrugs, though maybe she's just stretching. "To study. At Sophia, you know? I think you've heard of it. It's a pretty famous university."

"Yes," I say, though I can feel the muscles in my throat clenching. "I've seen pictures of it." I'm trying not to get my feet caught in the lengths of plastic tape, but there's so much of it, some of it wrapped around broken branches and rocks as if it's been arranged to trip people.

"Oh yeah? Well, I go there. A lot of my friends go there too. I think you might know a friend of mine."

"I don't think so."

"I do think so, Lily."

My legs stop working and there is no air in my lungs. Somewhere above me a bird calls, once, and then lapses back into silence.

"What did you call me?"

"You heard me fine."

I stop walking and push Mei against the trunk of a tree. I have no idea how to fight, but if I pretend like I do then maybe Mei will back off.

"Why did you bring me here, Mei? What do you want?"

I didn't realize how far we'd walked, and all I can see in every direction is the darkness of trees. I have no idea which direction would take me back to Hayati's car, and I'm not sure that's the safest place anyway.

"This is where the bodies are, Lily. I'm sorry it had to be like this, but it's the only way."

"What's the only way?"

"I want you to see. I need you to tell them."

Before I even know what's happening, Mei has grabbed hold of my hand and we're running through the trees faster than my feet will move. I'm stumbling over the broken plastic tape and I'm trying to shout out to Mei, questions and orders and curse words, but she just squeezes my hand so hard the bones grind together and pulls me along faster until black dots start pulsing in front of my eyes.

Thoughts are crashing through my head. This is the stupidest thing I have ever done. Liking the color of someone's hair is not reason enough to follow them into the forest of suicides. I remember the plots of every scary book I've ever read. All those stories about girls stumbling into dark basements, girls coming face-to-face with bad people who have done bad things, girls being saved by dashing men on horses. But those were just stories in books, and I'm in a forest full of dead people with a total stranger.

We break through into a clearing, and before my eyes can even focus, Mei has let go of my hand and disappeared off into the clumps of trees. The clearing is so silent that I can hear the thump of my heart and the rasp of my breath. Slowly the black dots clear from my vision, and I see a shoe. It's small and pink, a Chuck Taylor canvas sneaker. I start to move toward it when I realize that there's a foot in it.

I jerk back and look around the clearing, and I see more pink among the dead leaves, more shoes with more feet in them, more and more until I realize that there are a dozen bodies in the clearing. Bodies hanging from tree branches, bodies slumped against trunks, bodies stretched out on the ground like fallen logs.

My throat clenches shut as I realize that every body looks the same. Every body has my sister's face.

I close my eyes, but I can still see them. All those bodies. They're Cara, all of them. I open my mouth and I scream. I scream until I run out of breath and I'm just gasping at air, my hands over my eyes.

"Lily!" Mei is squeezing my wrists and shouting so hard her voice breaks, but the sound just gets swallowed up by the trees. "Stop it, please! Open your eyes!"

I stay still until I can breathe again, and then I open my eyes. The floor of the clearing is a mess of dead leaves and broken branches, but there are no pink sneakers, no feet, no bodies with Cara's face. I look all around, but Mei and I are the only ones here.

"I'm so sorry it had to be like this," says Mei. I don't want to listen to her, but I can't seem to move. "I didn't mean to upset you, but I knew that no other way would work. I've tried everything else, and this was the last—this was the only—I'm sorry, Lily."

"Take me home." I can hear the suppressed sobs in my voice, can feel the tears prickling my eyes, but I still hold Mei's gaze.

On the drive home Mei stares straight ahead but puts her arm behind her so I can take her hand if I want to. After an hour, I do.

She tells me what I already know: that Cara came over here to study three years ago, that she emailed us every week with messages and photos. That the messages got shorter, and shorter, and finally stopped. That she wouldn't answer the phone. That she was lonely and sad and couldn't cope with her work. That finally we moved over here to find her.

Then Mei tells me what I don't know: Cara walked into the forest a year ago and never came back. She left notes for everyone. Mei sent the note to my parents, and then she called them, and when she heard that we'd moved here, she went to visit. My parents wouldn't let her in. They said they hadn't gotten any note. They said they'd never heard of Mei, even though she'd been in many of the photos Cara had sent. She tried and tried to get them to accept the truth, but they said that if Mei came around again, they'd call the police. Then one day I came into the Starbucks at Shibuya. Mei recognized me from the family photos in Cara's room. She also recognized another chance to get my parents to accept the truth about Cara.

• • •

Back at home, my hands are shaking so much I can barely get the key to turn in the lock. For the first time in six months I don't take my shoes off at the door.

"Mum!" I run through the rooms, not stopping to hear her reply. "Mum!"

"Bloody hell, Lily! I'm right here." Mum emerges from the kitchen with her sleeves rolled up, something thick and beige coating her hands and wrists. "You're early, you're not meant to be here." Her eyes flick to the doorway of the other room. I don't know why, but she looks nervous. "Why are you back early? What do you…" She glances down at my shoes, then looks at me with her eyebrows raised. What is it about a mother's disapproval that can make your guts shrivel?

"I need to know where she is," I say.

"Who? What are you talking about? Seriously, Lily, you had better have a decent explanation for this. Your father is tired. You can't just come waltzing in here and…"

"*Cara*, Mum. Where is Cara?"

In books, characters always see emotions flicker across one another's faces. I can tell you now, that's total nonsense. I have no idea what emotions my mother is feeling; I just know that after a few seconds she turns away from me and goes into the kitchen and starts rinsing her hands in the sink. I follow her. I can hear from the sound of the water hitting the metal of the sink that her hands are shaking.

"I have to know," I say to her back.

"Go and see your father."

"Mum, I just want to…"

"GO AND—" Mum stops shouting, takes a deep breath out and in, and then adds in a quiet voice, "see your father."

In the other room, my dad is asleep on the couch. In front of him, the TV flickers.

"Dad, Mum said I should ask…"

I trail off when I see what's in his hand. It's a piece of paper. It looks like it's been torn from a notebook. The paper is thin and has been folded and refolded many times. I step across the room, feeling like I'm weightless, like all my internal organs have turned to air. I pluck the paper out of his hand.

Dear Mum, Dad, Lily,

I don't want to read it, but my eyes are going faster than my brain.

The most important thing to know is that I love you. I don't want you to think this is because of anything you did or didn't do. I knew I wouldn't be able to say goodbye to any of you, so this is how I am going to do it—in this letter, where you can't talk back or try to stop me. By the time you read this, I...

I tuck the paper back into my dad's hand. In the kitchen, the tap is still running.

"I know where she is," I say. The words come out as a whisper. I cough and try again. "I know where she is!"

Dad wakes with a jolt, his hand making a fist, crushing the paper. "Hunnhh," he says. In the kitchen, the tap stops running.

I wait until I can feel that Mum is standing in the doorway, and I say it again. "I know where Cara is. She's at Aokigahara."

Dad is still coming awake, but he seems to have gotten a handle on the situation surprisingly fast. "Lily, how do you...how could you know that?"

"I was there. Today. Tonight. Well, I don't really know what time it is, but I was there. I was with a friend of Cara's, an old friend."

"Did you see..." Mum can't even bear to finish the question.

"I didn't see her. But I know she's there."

Dad looks up at Mum, and for the first time, I'm aware of all the little lines around his eyes. "Perhaps we should go and bring her back. Her...her body."

"No!" I shudder from my scalp to my soles. "No, Dad. She doesn't want us to see her. Not like that. It's too late for that. Let's just...can we...please, can we go home?"

I don't understand why I can't say anything else, but then I see the tears dropping onto my shoes. Dad stands up and puts his arms around me; the pressure increases and I know Mum is holding me too. The paper gets crushed between us, and then it must fall to the floor because I can't see it anymore.

• • •

"Three hazelnut mochas, please," I say to the girl behind the counter at the Starbucks. I never see Mei in there anymore, but that's okay. We call each other once a week. Sometimes we talk about Cara, sometimes we just chat.

I lead Mum and Dad over to my usual seat, the one by the window. But this time, instead of looking out at all the faces going past, I turn my back to the window. I know that Cara is not out there.

I'll never stop missing her, but maybe the truth will help to bridge the gap that had been growing between my parents and me. Already it feels more like it used to be. Finally, I've realized that home can be anywhere, as long as I have my family with me. I lift my mocha and Mum clinks the rim of her cup against mine.

"Cheers," she says with a smile.

Kirsty Logan has visited many places and Tokyo is one of her favorites, though she has never been to Aokigahara. She currently lives in Scotland, where she writes fiction, edits magazine, reviews books, and works as an intern. She has a semicolon tattooed on her toe. Say hello at kirstylogan. com.

Submerged
by Elyse Dinh-McCrillis

I supposedly watched as my mother lay dying in a pool of her own blood in the middle of our living room. They found me crying, with my little hands leaving tiny red handprints on her face. I don't remember any of it, though. I was two years old.

But it all started coming back to me my senior year in high school, when I tried to bash a kid's head in with my book bag. Dad always said it was heavy enough to break someone's back, so I figured I'd use it to break stupid Vinnie's face. I had ignored him every time he called me names like "reject" and "loser" because, c'mon, those insults weren't even creative enough to get a rise out of me.

But I saw red when he called Billy a "'tard."

Billy was learning disabled; he was nineteen, but his intellect was equal to that of a fourteen-year-old. So he was a little old to be a freshman at our school, but he did just fine in his classes, especially math. Not like Vinnie, who was thirty or something and had been held back for twelve years because he was an idiot who couldn't locate Asia on a map and thought Huck Finn was some kind of fish.

I started out as Billy's tutor, but within days I considered him a friend. After our sessions, we'd go out to the school basketball court to shoot some hoops because Billy loved b-ball and that was his reward for solving his algebraic equations.

Then Vinnie came out that one day, laughed at Billy's lay-up attempts, and said, "Hey, look, 'tard playing basketball. Call the talent scouts!"

I didn't hesitate or say anything, just picked up my book bag and swung. I was aiming for Vinnie's head, but he was five foot ten to my five foot two so my bag, with my biology textbook inside, smashed into his ribs. When I swung a second time, I hit his kidney. Yeah, I actually read my biology book; I knew where the kidneys were. Vinnie said "Unnh" and went down like the piece of turd he was.

The next morning, Principal Stone suspended me until I completed ten sessions of counseling. And that's how I ended up on Dr. Taylor's couch. It's more like a La-Z-Boy, but she didn't let me recline.

"How's your situation at home?" Dr. Taylor asked.

"Fine."

"You live with your dad?"

"Yeah."

"Tell me about your mother."

Just like that.

"Oh, man!" I said, standing up. "Did Dad tell you to ask that?"

Dr. Taylor's eyes opened wide, but she didn't get up or raise her voice from that tone shrinks always used on TV.

"No, he didn't. I'm simply wondering if your mother is in the picture."

"Oh." I sat back down. But I didn't know how to talk about my mother, whose death I supposedly witnessed, the woman I could not remember.

"I never knew her. She died when I was two. But what's that got to do with anything?"

"I don't know what anything has to do with anything else until I hear the whole story."

"Great." I did a whole production of rolling my eyes, showing her only the whites. "We don't have enough time for the *whole* story."

"Okay, so let's just start with your mother."

People voluntarily pay for this?

I told her whatever I knew from what others had told me. Sixteen years ago, my dad came home from work and found my mother on the floor with me crying and holding on to her face. There were signs of a struggle, and it looked like she'd fallen through our glass coffee table. Our front door showed no sign of forced entry, and our neighbors heard and saw nothing. The case was unsolved. It took about five minutes to get through all that, which left forty-five more to fill until the end of the session.

"I see," Dr. Taylor said.

"Really? What do you see exactly?"

"I see that the situation with your mother may have resulted in your feeling that bad guys often go unpunished. I think it has more to do with why you lashed out at that boy at school than you realize."

I thought about that for a while. "That's stupid. It had nothing to do with my mother. I just gave dumb-ass Vinnie what he deserved."

"Maybe so, but I'd still like to learn more about what happened in your past. Long-buried feelings have a way of resurfacing…"

"I've already told you everything I know."

She smiled as if she were talking to an idiot, not at all miffed that I cut her off. "You'd be amazed by what we hold in our subconscious. Here's what I'd like you to do before our next session…"

"You're giving me *homework*?"

"Call it additional therapy. Write down everything you remember about your mother, even if it's something someone else told you. Start with a description. You must have seen pictures."

I rolled my eyes again, this time coming within millimeters of getting them permanently stuck in the back of my head.

"Okay, whatever. Can I go now?"

"Yes, I think it's okay for us to cut our first session short. See you next time."

• • •

That night, I sat in my room, looking through Mrs. Newman's window next door so I could watch *Columbo* on her TV. We didn't have the cable channel that carried TV classics. She had the volume turned up so loud, I could've heard the lieutenant say "And one more thing…" from space. And of course he got the perp to confess, like he always did. Why couldn't he have come around sixteen years ago to solve my mother's murder?

I looked down at the notebook I was supposed to be doing my therapy "homework" in, but as expected, I couldn't come up with anything to say about my mother that I hadn't already told Dr. Taylor. I got up and pulled a round metal tin out of the closet. It's a tin that used to hold Christmas cookies. After my dad and I ate them all, I kept the box because it's red and shiny and too pretty to throw away. It also smelled like cinnamon and sugar and made me feel like I was in someone's sepia-toned photograph every time I opened it. So I used it to store old photos, the ones that existed before digital cameras, like the ones of my mom holding a fat baby that didn't bear much resemblance to me except for the unruly hair.

I took one out and looked at it. Mom is smiling, pretending she's nibbling on my baby toes, her long dark hair in a ponytail with a few strays around her face. She doesn't look much older than I am now, though I know she was about twenty-seven when the picture was taken. She had a bright open face, the type that would encourage conversation if you sat next to her on a plane.

I stared at the photo for some time, trying to drag up some sense memory of being in her arms. My wide toothless baby grin was evidence of the joy and love I felt towards my mother—shouldn't that have left some kind of emotional footprint on me?

But nothing came. I could have been looking at an ad for baby food in a parenting magazine.

So I wrote a physical description of Mother in the notebook Dr. Taylor made me keep. It ended up being one paragraph, as brief as her life had been.

That night, I tossed and turned and had bizarre dreams. By the time I woke, with my brain as fuzzy as cotton, I couldn't recall my dreams but had this nagging feeling I should have remembered.

At the next session, Dr. Taylor asked me to read out loud what I'd written in my notebook. When I finished she said, "That's a good start. At least now I have a visual of her. Is there anything else you'd like to talk about?"

I wanted to change the topic and talk about school or Dad or stupid Vinnie or Billy. I was surprised to hear myself say, "I want to talk about Mother some more."

"All right. Did you remember something?"

"Uh, no. But I had these weird dreams right after I wrote in my notebook."

"What kind of dreams?"

"I couldn't remember, but I think they were trying to tell me something."

"Do you think they could be memories?"

"Memories of what?"

"I think you know."

"You mean *my mother*?" The chair wasn't so comfortable all of a sudden. "Do you really think so?" I looked at her, hoping she'd say no.

"It's possible. I don't think it's a coincidence that you started having these dreams right after we started talking about her."

"Oh, man, I don't think…I'm not sure I want to remember."

"Well, I certainly wouldn't want you to experience anything that might traumatize you. But I also think that remembering might also give you and your father closure. We'll just take it slow, see how much you can handle, and go from there, okay?" She smiled the kind of don't-panic smile that I'm sure was required before she was given a license to practice.

"Okay. I want to talk about something else now."

We spent the rest of the session discussing school and whether or not I was looking forward to going back. I missed attending classes. Morons like Vinnie aside, I liked school, everything from learning Mendel's peas theory about genetics to stories of the Round Table. And I missed tutoring Billy, but the school wouldn't let me near him until I'd completed my mandatory counseling for "anger management."

That night, after watching an old episode of *Barnaby Jones* via Mrs. Newman's window, I pulled another photo out of my cookie tin. But this was no Polaroid. It was black-and-white and on the front page of a newspaper.

The *Washington Sentinel* did an above-the-fold story on my mother's murder, using an archival photo they conveniently had of her from the previous year when she'd testified in a hit-and-run case that left a six-year-old local girl dead. The photographer caught Mother as she was walking up the courthouse stairs. She's looking at the camera, unsmiling but not uncomfortable. She wasn't posing for the photo, but she also had no problem being seen as the person who would put the drunk-driving bastard away.

That picture looked out of place, though, accompanying a story about Mother's own death. Usually, when someone dies tragically, you'd see a smiling photo of them in the media, on a beach or standing next to a Christmas tree, remnants of happier times. You don't often see photos of murder victims looking so serious.

I read the news story, but no new facts magically appeared. My mother was killed with me in the room, but I was left unhurt. Detective James Moran said the police had no suspects.

I had the bad dream again that night, this time sensing I was in a dark room and falling. And then I was on the floor looking at a pair of shoes. My heart was pounding wildly when I woke.

The dream happened a couple more times, each time with a few more details, so the following week I said to Dr. Taylor, "Can you help me recover my memories?"

Dr. Taylor looked at me for a moment before speaking. "I can, but are you ready to do that?"

"I don't know. I think all this talk about my mother is…shaking something loose. If I don't try to do something about it now, I may never remember."

"How do you feel about hypnosis?"

"I…have no idea. I've never tried it."

"Would you be open to it? The more you believe in its potential, the higher the chances are that it will work."

I didn't think about it very long. "When can we do it?"

Dr. Taylor said she didn't do hypnosis herself but would refer me to someone she trusted. She gave me a name and number, told me to set it up and she would meet me there.

• • •

The day of the session, I showed up with Dad at an address that looked like someone's house. When I rang the doorbell, a man in his forties opened the door instantly, as if he had been standing on the other side waiting for me. Creepy.

"Hello, you must be Jamie and Mr. Ford," he said.

"Uh, yeah. Is Dr. Taylor here yet?"

"No, but I expect her shortly."

"Are you Arthur Dale?" Dad said.

"Yes, I am. Welcome."

He stepped back, smiled, and opened the door wider, which made me feel *less* welcome for some reason. He led us into a living room that had been converted into a waiting room, with leather chairs so shiny you could stare into their surface to apply makeup.

He kept walking and took us to a small inner office that was furnished in pretty much the same style as the waiting room. This dude had money. Whether or not he could help me remained to be seen.

"Have a seat," Dale said. Dad and I remained standing. He smiled again, then sat down first. "As you wish."

Just then, his doorbell rang.

Dale stood back up. "That must be Dr. Taylor."

Finally, I thought, but said, "You want me to get it?"

"No, that's quite all right. I'll get the door. Make yourself comfortable."

Dad and I sat on a couch, but we didn't lean all the way back.

"Is that a stuffed squirrel?" Dad asked, indicating something on Dale's bookshelf.

"I don't want to know, Dad."

We didn't say anything else. I started playing with a snow globe of Vegas I saw on a side table.

Two minutes later, Dale led Dr. Taylor into the room. She was dressed in jeans and looked smaller and younger than she usually did in her office. I introduced Dad to her, and we all made small talk. Dr. Taylor told stories about other clients she had sent to Dale, people whom he'd helped remember past trauma or quit smoking, etc. She never made a hard sell, leaving the ultimate decision up to me. I finally decided that, stuffed squirrels and Vegas snow globes aside, Dale could try to put me under.

After I signed a waiver that said I wouldn't sue Dale if he scrambled my brain, he told me to sit in a chair that reclined. He pulled his chair next to mine and spoke softly. "All right, Jamie, relax and listen to my voice. You're feeling really good right now, you're perfectly safe, just focus on my words…"

I was sitting there thinking there was no way this was going to work when I found myself in an unfamiliar room, sitting on the floor. How did I fall out of the chair? I heard a really awful noise that sounded like a cat squealing and realized it was coming from me. And I seemed to have the hiccups. I was heading towards something, but things were too fuzzy and too big and too sharp. And then I saw the shoes again, the same ones I'd seen before. The shoes were attached to feet that were attached to pants. I clutched at the pants leg and tried to stand up. I looked up, asking for help, but nothing came out of my mouth except more wailing. The pants leg didn't move but then someone was bending down…

Next thing I knew, I was back in Dale's office and sobbing hard. Dad was crouching next to me, holding my hand, looking scared. Dr. Taylor was also there, giving me concerned eyes but not touching me or saying anything.

"You're okay, Jamie. Everything is fine. Everything is okay," Dale was murmuring.

But it wasn't okay. I had seen something that terrified me, and I cried because I knew I would have to go back in and face the rest.

• • •

A week later, I tried again. This time, I saw more.

I snapped my eyes open and gasped for air. In a flash, Dad was there, rocking me the way he used to when I was five. I squeezed my eyes shut and held on tight, shaking as if I'd just plunged off a cliff into icy cold water. And maybe I had, because I finally remembered something that had long been submerged.

Dad helped me out of the chair and told Dale and Dr. Taylor we were going home. We stayed up talking through the night about what I should do. I recalled seeing the name of the detective on the case in the newspaper article and thought it was time we called him. Dad resisted the idea, but ultimately agreed I could contact Detective Moran in the morning.

When the time came, though, I found myself staring at the phone, not sure what I'd say to him. "Hi, I might have some information about my mother's murder sixteen years ago"? And then tell him it came to me through dreams and hypnosis? How quickly would he hang up on me?

But I knew I had to at least try, so with unsteady hands, I dialed the Oakton police department and asked for Detective Moran. I was put on hold for a long time and was just about to hang up when the line was picked up again.

"Moran." He sounded like the man with a hole in his throat in that commercial telling you not to smoke.

"Hi, Detective Moran, I, uh…"

"Who is this?"

"I'm…my name is…" I stopped, took a deep breath and started over.

"My name is Jamie Ford, I'm Julia Ford's daughter. You investigated her case when she was murdered in 1995. Do you remember it?"

There was a long pause at the other end. Then: "Yeah, I remember. Woman killed while her baby watched." I flinched, but he couldn't see.

He cleared his throat. "I guess that would be you. What can I do for you?" His voice a little quieter and less scary. I plowed on.

"I think I have information that might help you solve the case."

"Where did you get this information?"

"It…I stumbled across it. Going through some of her things." Well, that's how it had started, with the old photos in the cookie tin.

"What exactly is it?"

"I don't want to tell you over the phone. Can we discuss it in person? I can come down—"

"I'll come to you. Are you still at the old place?"

"Um, no. We moved after…well, after." I rattled off our new address.

"Five P.M. I'll stop by after my shift." He hung up.

I flipped my cell closed and called Dad at work. "He's coming at five."

"You want me there?"

I considered that a moment, then told him what I thought. Dad didn't like it, but I convinced him it was the best way to go.

At 4:50, the knocker rapped against our front door. I opened it and saw the man from that faded old newspaper photo staring back at me. His face had filled out a little but hadn't lost its sharpness. His hair was sprinkled with gray but he looked better for it. He would have been what my friends and I called a hottie if he didn't have such sad eyes.

"Detective Moran?"

"Ms. Ford?"

"Uh, Jamie."

I opened the door wider and he stepped inside. His eyes never left my face.

"Last time I saw you, you were a baby."

"So I've heard."

"You're eighteen now?"

"Yeah."

"Wow." He seemed to be thinking about something, but then shook it off.

"Is your dad home?"

"No, he's at work."

I led him through the French doors and out to where the pool was. It was a nice warm day and the backyard was always my sanctuary when

I felt stressed about something. I thought the view would help while I shared my dark secrets with Detective Moran.

I offered him water or one of my dad's beers, but he shook his head.

"Just tell me about this new evidence you found."

I told him about my hypnosis sessions and how I was recalling more with each one, that the last time I went under I'd finally seen a face in the same room with my mother the night she died. The face was a little blurry, but I could tell it was a man with brown hair and slender build. I thought the murderer was someone my mother knew, because the overall sensation I had in these memories was that my mother wasn't scared until right before she died.

"So let me get this straight. You didn't find any actual evidence. You're just having dreams and feelings?"

"They're not just dreams. It's like I'm unlocking something my subconscious had blocked because I couldn't handle it before. But I think I can deal with it now. It still scares me a little, but I feel like I have to do this. I think it will all come back to me in the next few sessions, but things are still fuzzy. I was wondering if maybe you could let me look at the file on my mother's case. Maybe it would help me remember more."

"When's your next session?"

"Tomorrow morning."

He didn't say anything for a minute, just sat there unmoving. It was so quiet I could hear the hum of the pool filter. Then Detective Moran seemed to come to some sort of decision.

"All right, you can look at the file at the station tomorrow. We can go through the list of people of interest back then and see if I should take a look at one of them again."

"Okay."

We stood up at the same time, and he reached out with his right hand. I thought he was going to shake mine. Instead, he caught me by my shoulder and threw me into the deep end of the pool. I quickly went under, swallowing water all the way since my mouth was still O-shaped in surprise.

I kicked when I reached bottom, but just as I surfaced and managed to gulp in a lungful of air, Moran was beside me in the pool, pushing my head back under. I started kicking and clawing, but underwater my efforts were feeble. I tried to scratch at his arms, but he didn't even flinch. I looked up at him through the water and thought I could hear him saying "I'm sorry" over and over, but that couldn't have been right. My brain was deprived of oxygen.

My arms were getting tired from struggling when I saw Mother. Her face came to me, smiling, and she was saying something to me, too. Maybe I could float over to her and she'd give me a hug and things would be okay and…

There was a loud noise and the force holding me below water was gone. I kicked to the surface and gulped like a baby taking its first breath. Then Dad's arms were around me, rocking me in that familiar way. "It's okay, baby, it's over," he said.

He held me while I coughed, and after a while my body calmed. I looked over and saw Moran floating facedown, blood trickling from his head. There was a baseball bat at the bottom of the pool.

"I'm sorry it took me so long to come downstairs," Dad said.

"It's okay. You made it."

We pulled Detective Moran over to the side of the pool and heaved him up and over. He came to, but Dad kicked him in the head and he went out again. I flashed to Dr. Taylor telling me that my trying to bash in Vinnie's head may have had something to do with what happened to Mother. I was thinking maybe I got it from Dad.

The story unfolded over the next few days in the media. A sixteen-year-old cold case that finally gets solved is big news. But Dad and I didn't answer any of the requests for interviews from local papers and TV stations.

Moran had been the lead detective on the hit-and-run case my mother testified in as a witness. After many hours spent interviewing and seeing her in court, he fell in love with her, but she rebuffed his advances. He came to our house, drunk, the evening she died, hoping to change her mind. There was a struggle, and he accidentally pushed her back into our glass coffee table. He left, sobered up, and returned hours later as the lead detective on her killing. He knew I'd been a witness but was sure that two-year-olds don't have lasting memories. He thought he'd gotten away with it until he received my phone call. Then he panicked.

I didn't know all that, but I did know it was him after my second session with Arthur Dale. I had seen Moran's face but had no proof of his guilt. The plan had been to invite him over and have Dad come home early from work and watch from the upstairs window to see what Moran would do. I also had the record function on my iPhone going in case he said something incriminating. We never expected him to react so fast and so violently. What a couple of amateurs we were.

Other stories eventually replaced ours in the news, and I went back to school. It was a little weird at first because kids who had never talked to me before suddenly started treating me like I was a star from a reality show. Vinnie kept his distance. After bruising his ribs and kidney, I'd been involved in another incident in which a veteran police officer was almost killed. No way was Vinnie messing with me.

I no longer had to go to counseling, but I kept seeing Dr. Taylor anyway. And even though she stopped asking about my mother, I couldn't stop talking about her.

Elyse Dinh-McCrillis is a former news reporter who currently works as an actress/writer/editor. She blogs about books, movies, and TV at Pop Culture Nerd (popculturenerd.com). She proudly admits to playing chess and knowing every line of dialogue from *Star Wars*.

Falsely Accused
by KC Sprayberry

The humid, sticky, August heat pressed against nineteen-year-old Bec Janson. Despite a deep desire to sprawl under an air conditioner until she left for Southern Georgia University next week, Bec strolled along Duke Street. She and her friends were on a mission to solve a mystery that was over a hundred years old before they left for college.

A popular teen throughout high school, Bec had a short cap of honey-blonde hair that curled around her face. Wide-set gray/green eyes and freckles set off her petite nose. She smiled as she wondered how the adults in her life would view their quest. She wore a pair of white shorts and a bright green tank top with kicks and no socks in an effort to remain cool as she hunted for clues to the lost treasure.

"We're nuts," Bec muttered to herself as she waved at a woman dragging a wheeled garbage can to the curb. "No one's ever found any evidence that the Tremaine fortune even existed."

All the arguments she had used last night echoed in her head, but Bec shook off logic in the bright morning sunlight. The money had vanished months before the Civil War began, and the currency was now worthless, except to collectors. Jason Tremaine, the newspaper publisher, had recently reignited interest in the mystery by offering a $35,000 reward for anyone who came up with a viable clue as to how the money disappeared. After reading the article online several times, Bec realized that finding the money wasn't necessary, just a clue as to where it went and who took it.

"All anyone really knows is that the money probably never left Landry," Bec said. "There was a typhus outbreak that had the entire county quarantined."

Several school buses rumbled past, the students looking anything but happy about returning to school in the oppressive heat.

"Hey, Bec!" a girl called. "You lucky dog. Sure wish I was going to college this year."

"Have fun today, Keisha." Bec smiled at Keisha Carson, the youngest member of her crew. "We'll think of you while we're looking for the money."

Keisha's father was her father's oldest friend. Keisha wrinkled her button nose at Bec and flounced back into her seat as the bus approached a stoplight at the corner of Duke and Villanow Road. Other teens had teased them about the treasure hunt, but Bec's excitement had only grown.

"A treasure hunt." Bec giggled. "That does sound exciting."

The money had disappeared a long time ago, and there was no guarantee, of course, that anyone would ever find it. Her friends had pledged to donate the reward to a local center for women—if they managed to find the treasure.

A dark gray sedan cruised past Bec and she grinned. Inside the car were her dad, Adam Janson, who was Wallis County's district attorney, and Mike Carson, Keisha's dad, the deputy sheriff assigned to Adam to work pre-trial investigations. The Carsons had made Bec part of their family following the death of her mother sixteen years ago from cancer. The families lived next-door to each other and were always visiting back and forth.

Bec swung onto Villanow Road and walked with long, sure strides toward the highway on Landry's outer edge. Her job this morning was to check out a couple of abandoned houses near the Quick Stop. Bec had called the owner last night to get her permission to enter the empty buildings. She was sure she would find nothing but dust and spiders during her time inside the old homes. They were like a half dozen others in town that had been built in the early nineteenth century and might hold a clue as to where the Tremaine fortune could be or who might have taken the money. Tremaine had been known for banning slavery in this town at a time when most of the South believed otherwise.

"This is bogus," Bec thought as she stopped across from the first house and stared at the dilapidated white wood-frame building. "No one left anything worth finding in there."

Just as she was about to cross the street, her cell phone rang. Bec glanced at the caller ID and smiled.

"Hey, Ev," she said in a soft voice. "Ready to admit this is the wrong day to do this?"

Evan Tinker, known to his friends as Ev, laughed. He was much taller than Bec's five foot, four inches, and had played football on the Junior Varsity team. His biggest triumph in high school had been leading the baseball team to a state championship two months ago. His dark blonde hair was cut short, and his blue eyes fascinated Bec. They weren't the standard faded blue, but the blue of a late-winter sky before a storm, and capable of being cold and harsh, as well as warming the person he turned his gaze upon. Not long before Christmas, Ev and Bec began dating, an experience she welcomed after several attempts to find a guy who did not want to mess around on the first date.

"Not the wrong day at all," Ev said. "It's a perfect day to grub around in old houses looking for clues. Why are you so down on this? You're usually the one who demands we take on the tough stuff."

"This time it feels different," Bec said. "I can't explain it, but I feel like something bad is about to happen."

"Nothing bad will happen," Ev said. "I need a favor."

"What?"

Bec started to cross the street hoping this favor would not keep her out in the heat any longer than necessary.

"Lane called," he said. "He, Vic, and Kris found something last night that might lead us to the treasure."

Her first instinct was to cringe. Lane Miller had asked Bec out during football season. She had gone out with him a grand total of three times. Then she broke the relationship off after Lane pressured her to have sex with him. He had even gone so far as to refuse to take her home until long after midnight on their last date. Not that she was a prude of anything like that but Bec wanted a guy who gave her a feeling of safety and caring and not "let's jump in the sack" whenever they went out. Even creepier was how his best buds, Kris Jackson and Vic Escalante, always showed up wherever Lane took her. No one ever saw one without the others being close by, it seemed.

"And your point is?" Bec checked the street, then ran across after seeing no traffic. "Lane creeps me out." She stared at the falling-down house. "Why didn't Lane give you the 411 over the phone? How did he even know to call you? It's not like we told anyone what we're doing."

A sense of unease surrounded Bec. She couldn't shake the feeling that something bad was about to happen. Whenever Lane tried to shove his way back into her life, she felt like this. This time, the feeling was even stronger.

"He said his dad heard about what we're doing," Ev said. "Lane promised to give you the paper his dad found in their basement. No pressure. No hard time about you breaking things off with him. Come on, Bec. It won't take long."

That might have happened, but Bec had her doubts. Lane's dad worked with hers, he was an assistant district attorney. But Bob Miller wasn't one of her dad's confidants. Still...it might be the truth.

"Did Lane say what this paper is that his dad found?" she asked.

"A map," Ev said. "Supposedly a map of a network of tunnels. They're under those old houses up at the lake. Can you check it out? Lane's at the Quick Stop right now. I know you're close by if you're already on the search."

"I am." Bec looked away from the house and stared in the direction of Highway 27.

A series of tunnels under the historic houses by the lake? None of the stories about Landry had ever mentioned such a thing. Bec looked over the house she had to search and shuddered when she spotted a bunch of very large spiderwebs draped around the door. Putting up with Lane for ten minutes was a lot better than knocking down those webs. The spiders that had made them were nowhere in sight, but her imagination conjured up massive eight-legged creatures attacking her as soon as she ripped down their homes.

"All right," Bec said. "Call you when I know what Lane has."

"Thanks," Ev said. "I knew I could count on you."

Bec slid her phone into a pocket of her shorts and walked back to the street. The sidewalk was cracked and there were lots of pieces of concrete that threatened to trip her. She concentrated on maintaining her balance as she made her way to the Quick Stop. Lane's Mustang sat in front of the gas pumps, and she hurried over.

"Where's the map?" Bec asked, ignoring Southern protocol that demanded she talk about any number of issues before coming to her point. Getting away from Lane before he made a nasty comment was her only mission. Maybe, if she accomplished this task fast, she would have a chance to return to her original plans without any problems.

"Give me a hand." Lane stuck the nozzle of the gas pump into his

1965 cherry-red Ford Mustang as his buds, Vic and Kris, went into the store. "Kris thought I had a taillight out. I need to check that before we go up to the lake." Lane tossed her the keys. "Give me a chance to gas up first, then turn on the car and step on the brake when I tell you."

"Fine." Bec got behind the wheel. "Where's the map?"

"Between the front seats," Lane said.

She stuck the key in the ignition and found the map. Without taking time to look it over, Bec shoved the old paper into her shorts pocket and rolled her eyes. This was definitely taking longer than she wanted.

A few minutes later, Lane hung up the gas pump and walked around to the back of the vehicle. Bec put her hand on the key.

"Hurry up," she muttered. "I don't have all day."

The sun beat down on her head and sweat poured down her skin. Bec started to turn around and yell at Lane about taking his time when he slapped the trunk.

"Turn it on," Lane called.

Bec turned the key. The car roared to life. She stepped on the brake and waited for Lane to tell her he had found the problem.

"What's—"

A loud bang and the sound of glass shattering interrupted her question. Bec glanced over her shoulder to see Kris and Vic race out of the store. Both were holding guns. Lane pulled a weapon from the waistband of his jeans and the three guys started shooting at the store. Shocked, Bec grabbed the door handle, but they dove into the car.

"Drive!" Lane shouted. "Get out of here now!"

He grabbed the gearshift and pulled it into drive. The car leapt forward and Bec held on to the steering wheel to maintain control. Her foot moved toward the brake pedal as she reached for the door handle. Lane straddled the small space between the seats and jammed his foot down on the accelerator.

"Turn onto the highway." Lane pressed the gun against her ribs. "Don't try anything or you'll regret it."

The gun's muzzle made a sharp pain radiate up and down her right side. Bec swung the car onto the street and narrowly avoided a speeding truck. The blare of a horn accompanied her as she raced along the highway. Lane pushed harder and harder against her until they shared the cramped seat. The door's handle bit into her left hip and Bec wondered if he would shove her out at some point. She hoped not. At this speed road rash would be the least of her problems.

"Thanks for nothing." Lane slowed the vehicle and reached across her to open the door. "Have a nice trip." He cackled. "This is for dumping me!"

Hands from the back seat propelled Bec to the left, and she flew over the patch of road, hitting the grassy embankment and rolling until she landed in a muddy ditch. Sputtering and spitting mud, she came to her knees and stared in disbelief at the rear of the Mustang as it turned off on a dirt road and vanished from sight.

"They robbed the Quick Stop." Shock settled in as Bec's muscles resembled a half-set bowl of Jell-O. "And I helped."

The implications, whether or not she knew about the robbery beforehand, slammed into Bec. Her dad was a law-and-order kind of guy. This might just be the worst situation in his life since losing his wife sixteen years ago.

"OMG!" Bec took a shaky breath as sirens echoed from every direction. "Lane left me here to get caught."

She could think of only one place that might offer sanctuary until she could figure out how to explain the situation. Ev's dad had a house on the lake, the same house where tonight almost a hundred teens would congregate to celebrate before heading to college next week. After the treasure hunt, Bec was supposed to make sure everything for the barbecue was in place, but now she needed the house to hide in until everything quieted down.

"Please, Dad, understand." She looked around and groaned. Between her and the safety of a heavily wooded forest was a field of unmown hay. She was sure to be spotted as she ran through the tall scratchy stalks.

The sound of a high-powered engine made Bec duck as a sheriff's cruiser raced past. A quick peek over the embankment confirmed that the deputy was headed for the Quick Stop. There were already more cops there than she had ever seen in one place in her entire life. One thing was missing and her heart skipped a beat. No ambulance meant the owner, Mr. Singh, might have died in the encounter. He may have survived without injury, but three out-of-control teens firing guns into plate-glass windows ensured at least an injury. Bec's overactive imagination conjured up images of the quiet Indian owner lying sprawled in a growing puddle of blood.

"I'm sorry," she whispered. "If I'd known—"

She *had* known, in a weird way. The sense that something was wrong had bothered her all morning. Lane had sworn he would get even with Bec after their breakup. She always thought Lane would just start a bunch of rumors about her. This was so much worse.

Before her eyes, cop car after cop car raced past until it looked like every officer in Georgia was outside the Quick Stop. The crackle of so many radios made it hard to understand what they were saying, but Bec was sure of one thing. They wanted her. She heard her name more than once. Certain no one aligned with her dad would believe her story, she crawled out of the ditch and crept into the hay field. Panic set in and she ran, creating a wide swath, but she didn't slow down until she reached the woods. Bec stopped to catch her breath and saw several state patrol cars slow down near the ditch she had just left, and she took off with even greater panic.

She crashed through the woods and onto the lake's beach. Thankfully, no one was around. She didn't see anyone at the windows of the houses lining the lake. She ran as if the devil himself was pursuing her and didn't stop until she was inside Ev's dad's lake house. The sound of a foot scuffing the slate floor made her jump, and her heart leapt into her throat.

"What's up?" Ev asked as if nothing in the world had happened. "Did you get the map?"

"The map." Bec touched her shorts pocket. "Yeah, I got the map." She faced Ev and discovered the rest of her friends were there. "And something else. You promised Lane wouldn't try anything, Ev." Tears started rolling down her face. "He did! Damn you for convincing me to meet them! Lane, Kris, and Vic robbed the Quick Stop. They made me drive them away!"

Her friends stared at her in horror. Jack Winders, the sheriff's son, yanked out his cell phone and turned his back. Seconds later, she heard him talking to his dad.

"You're kidding. Right?" Dy Andrews asked.

Dy was Jack's girlfriend and although they had recently announced their engagement, their plan was to wait to wed until after they both graduated from SGU. An inch taller than Bec, Dy had glorious white-blonde hair and deep blue eyes. Her slender form came from hours of playing tennis. Dy and Bec had been best friends since before Bec's mom died.

"No." Bec shook her head. "Lane forced me to drive. I tried to get away. Really, I did. But he, he…" Bec start to shake again. "He used a gun on me. He shoved a gun into my ribs and made me drive away before he pushed me out on the highway."

Shocked gasps greeted her story. Ev moved across the room and enveloped Bec in a tight hug.

"We believe you," Ev said. "No matter what Lane and his creepy friends say, we know you'd never help anyone rob a store."

"There's more." Bec sobbed. "I think they killed Mr. Singh. Lane, Vic, and Kris were shooting through that big front window. Then they jumped into Lane's car and made me drive."

"She's right," Jack said. "The cops want to talk to Bec, but Dad wouldn't say why. All he told me was that she was considered dangerous and possibly armed. There was a witness, a truck driver that she cut off when leaving the store."

"I tried to stop, but Lane had the gun in my ribs and slammed his foot down on the accelerator." Bec stepped away from Ev and carefully lifted her shirt. A bright red mark outlined the gun's muzzle perfectly against several ribs. "See?"

"That's—" Dy covered her mouth with a hand.

"OMG!" Rika Thompson exclaimed as she hugged Tomas Aleriti. "It's true. He really forced you. No one would ever do that to themself."

A quiet girl interested in freeform painting, Rika had surprised everyone at graduation by taking the top honors for their class. Her tall, slender figure shrank as Tomas held her tightly. Dark brown hair and hazel eyes stared at Bec from a face twisted in shock and anger. Tomas, a Puerto Rican, frowned. At six feet, he had played baseball with Ev and planned to become a paramedic after finishing college.

"Jack, you have to convince your dad to back off. Fast. Bec needs to tell her side of the story first," Cam Switzer said.

A Francophile, Cam's red hair ended in waves at her shoulders. She wore black Capris with a diagonally striped white and black oversized t-shirt. A black beret was perched on one side of her head.

"Probably won't happen that way," Will Breeker commented. "What else, Jack? What aren't you telling us?"

The most settled member of their crew, Will had announced he would major in police science with Jack at SGU. Both planned to work in Landry one day, Jack as police chief and Will as sheriff.

"Mr. Singh died," Jack said. "From the video and truck driver's statement, it looked like Bec helped. She started Lane's ride while he stood lookout and Vic and Kris robbed the store."

"It wasn't like that!" Bec cried. "Lane said one of his taillights was out. He wanted me to start the car and step on the brakes so he could check it after he pumped gas. I swear! I'm telling the truth."

"Then we have to prove that to the cops," Ev said. "Where's the map?"

The map? He still wanted to search for the Tremaine fortune after everything that had happened this morning? Bec jerked the map from her pocket and thrust it at him.

"Here," she snapped. "But I have to say, this is lousy timing. I don't care about that Treamine fortune any more. All I want to do is prove I didn't help those losers."

Bec couldn't believe that they still wanted to find the treasure despite what she faced. All thoughts of fun in college fled as Bec imagined a future filled with her arrest, trial, and imprisonment. She was the district attorney's daughter! This couldn't happen to her.

"Don't freak," Dy said in a breathless voice. "It's not what you think. Jack's dad believes Lane's posse drove over to the lake. If Lane knows the map, if he doesn't need it, they might go into those tunnels he told Ev about. Right?" She turned to Jack. "That's why we're looking at the map instead of figuring out how to help Bec. Tell me it is."

"It is." Jack stared at Bec. "Dad doesn't know where we are. He suspects you're with us, so we're all in trouble if we don't find Lane, Kris, and Vic fast." He took in each of the others with a glance. "And I do mean *deep* trouble. Trouble as bad as Bec unless we catch those jerks and turn them over to the cops."

Jack forgot to mention one thing, something that bothered Bec a lot.

"But Lane will say I was part of it all along," Bec cried. "He's still pissed about me dumping him. That's what he said when he pushed me out of the car."

"Then we'll prove him wrong," Jack said. "Listen Bec, your dad and mine are going over the survelience tape right now. I heard Mike Carson say it didn't look like you were cooperating. They could see Lane crawling into the driver's seat with you, and Mike wanted a blow-up of one second of the getaway. He said something about seeing Lane's arm moving in a strange way."

Bec took a deep breath and tried to calm down. They had a chance, but only if Lane, Kris, and Vic were stupid enough to hide the loot from the robbery in the tunnels.

"What if Lane isn't in the tunnels?" Bec asked. "What if those tunnels don't exist? We're taking a huge chance. The rest of you can take off and I'll call Dad and try to explain. Maybe I'll have to wait a couple of years to go to college, but not if we don't call my dad now."

The others shook their heads. Ev held out the map.

"This isn't old," Ev said. "It's supposed to look old, but the paper's not thin enough for a map from before the Civil War. I think I know where they may have gone."

"Where?" Bec snatched the map and looked over an elaborate tunnel system under houses surrounding the lake.

Only most of these houses didn't exist anymore, and the rest of them were nothing more than falling-down shacks now. Their chance of finding the right entrance, and following it to the spot where a circle highlighted a section of the tunnel, was slim to zero. Bec was willing to take that chance. She would take any chance to find Lane before the police caught up with her.

"Okay." She nodded. "I guess we should start with the shack closest to us." Bec looked at Ev. "But it is across an open road. We have to figure out a way to avoid the cops."

The other shack was out of the question as it was on the far side of the lake. They would waste too much time sneaking around in the woods trying to avoid anyone still in their houses.

"We can do it." Will checked out a window. "It's only half a mile away. We will stay in the woods until we get close, and then we sprint."

A short sprint was nothing. Still, Bec hoped no one would notice her out in the open. With her friends behind her, she had a chance to prove the truth, but not if they got caught.

"Let's go." Bec raced for the door. "We don't have much time."

Bec no longer cared about a treasure hunt. She only wanted to prove her innocence and get on with her life.

At first, the race for the abandoned shack seemed like a footrace. Bec remained in the lead, until Ev jerked her behind a tree. Jack and Dy crept out onto the dirt road and looked in all directions. There were several vacation homes there, but it appeared as if no one was in them. After a few minutes, Dy waved the rest of the group out. Cam, Will, Rika, and Tomas surrounded Bec and Ev as they moved across the road. Every step brought heart-thumping terror as Bec thought about the cops who wanted to talk to her, as a suspect. Never had she thought she would be in this position.

"Relax." Ev grabbed her wrist once they were across the road. He looked down. "Where's your bracelet?"

"What?" Bec stared at bare skin where a medic-alert bracelet advised people she was allergic to chamomile. There was nothing there. "OMG! When did I lose the bracelet?"

She had only had one attack when she was six, but remembered all too well the runny nose and stomach cramps that escalated into hives and breathing problems. Rika's dad, Monty, had figured out the allergic reaction before Bec stopped breathing, but now she lived in fear of even brushing up against a chamomile plant.

"Relax," Rika said. "If you do find a chamomile plant in these woods, I'll call Dad. He'll come and won't say where you are."

"He won't have to," Bec said in complete misery. "There won't be time."

"Then you won't come into contact with chamomile," Ev said. "We'll be extra careful."

Bec didn't want to be extra careful. She just wanted to find the money and prove she hadn't robbed the Quick Stop. The others started walking again. Bec focused on the shack, listing to one side, that laid ahead of them. To her horror, near the door was a plot of wild chamomile. The leafy green plant boasted a full growth of yellow flowers, and a stink filled the air. These plants were in full bloom and were an extreme danger to Bec.

"Just our luck." Jack shook his head. "What now?"

"The other shack," Ev said. "We'll have to take a chance on getting around the lake. Come on, guys. We can't hang around here all day. Your dad will get suspicious soon, Jack, if we don't check in like you promised."

Bec backed away from the dangerous chamomile, and they were soon on the road. The sound of four-wheelers sent the teens racing into the woods without looking, but Bec kept a good eye out for more of the wild chamomile. The plant was worse than dandelions and could spread all over the place.

"Duck!" Tomas called in a hoarse voice.

"Incoming," Rika warned. "And it looks like…" She knelt in the weeds around the trees. "Lane and his pals!"

Bec and Ev crouched close to the ground in a clearing while the others lurked behind trees and peered around bushes. Lane, Kris, and Vic drove past without looking at them. A sigh of relief escaped Bec as the losers disappeared.

"They're not going toward any of the houses on the map." Ev stood. "Come on. We have to catch up with them. I bet Lane didn't put everything on this map."

Just their luck. Bec snuck through the trees and bushes with her crew as Lane stopped at a modern, single story house near the lake. He, Kris, and Vic got off the four-wheelers and looked around. Seconds later, they pulled up what looked like a wooden pallet and disappeared into the ground.

"What?" Will crawled out. "Hang on until I check this out."

After what seemed like forever, Will pulled up the wooden pallet and vanished inside a large hole. One of his hands rose into the air and he waved the others forward. They raced across the open area, where anyone on the lake could see them, and stopped beside Will.

"It's a passageway," Will said. "I can hear Lane talking. He's bragging about how Bec's in trouble but no one's identified them yet."

"Proof enough to get the cops started this way?" Jack looked at Ev.

"It'll have to be." Ev pulled Bec into a sideways hug. "We can't risk Bec running into any chamomile around here and we can't have the cops showing up without calling. Tell your dad the whole story, Jack."

The guys started arguing. Dy, Cam, and Rika joined in, but Bec wanted no more wasted time. Her entire life hung in the balance. One way or another, she would find the necessary proof and make Lane confess.

Sure hope Lane doesn't still have that gun. Bec grimaced at the thought. *He probably threw the gun away wherever he hid his car.*

Bec lowered herself into the passageway and started creeping along the damp earth. With her back to the wall, she concentrated on Lane's voice ahead of her. The sound of kicks hitting the ground startled her and she glanced over her shoulder. Ev ran over to her.

"You should have waited." Ev scooted in front of Bec. "You can't go in there alone, Bec. Lane almost killed you this morning."

"And he wants me to go to prison," Bec whispered. "That is *so* not happening." She moved close to Ev. "But they haven't said if they have the money in here."

"We'll have to take that chance," Ev said. "Jack's talking to his dad now. The others stayed outside to give us a couple of minutes."

"They may not have it." Bec stared at the still open entrance. "I hear sirens."

The muffled sound of sirens raced toward them. Fear pushed Bec to take chances, but Ev held onto her arm as they crept along the tunnel. Rotting beams bracing the ceiling creaked and groaned as the heavy vehicles roared past. When she and Ev heard angry voices, Bec shivered with fear.

"This isn't happening," she said. "I won't quit until I know why."

She already knew why Lane had involved her, even asking Ev to have Bec to pick up the supposed map, but she wanted to know why three guys with lots of money had robbed a convenience store and killed the owner. Ev nodded and pushed her behind his back while moving to the small cave where Lane, Kris, and Vic laughed.

"That stupid bitch never saw it coming," Lane bragged. "All she could think about was the Tremaine fortune. Well, this is the only fortune I'm interested in. We have enough to score some beer."

"Not really." Kris rustled a hand through the bag. "There's probably less than three hundred here. We should have made the jerk open his safe instead of running off."

"The jerk had a baseball bat," Vic said. "I wasn't going to let him chase us and maybe call the cops before we could blame Clueless." He barked out a laugh. "Did you see the look on her face when you shoved her out of your car, Lane? Bec looked like she was about to die! I checked the scanner while we hid the Mustang. The cops want her. They don't know who we are, but they sure got a full picture of Bec. She's going away for what we did."

Bec burned with anger. None of them had changed one bit from the fools she remembered from when she had dated Lane. No, they were worse. Far worse.

"Do you see the money?" Bec whispered to Ev.

"It's in there." Ev moved aside. "And we're out of here. It's time to send in the real cops."

She almost giggled, but instead she focused on the small cave where Lane, Kris, and Vic sat and concentrated on the small white plastic bag with "Quick Stop" in red letters across it. It was almost flat, with only a little bit of money in the bottom. Bec sucked in a breath of relief and pulled Ev toward the entrance. They took three steps before she stared in disbelief at a wall of very angry looking cops.

"They're back there." Bec pointed at the small cave. "Lane Miller, Kris Jackson, and Vic Escalante robbed the store. I didn't know what was going on. Really." She gulped when her dad's angry face came into view. "I didn't know, Dad."

"Outside." Mike Carson grabbed Bec's arm and signaled Ev to get in front of him. "Both of you. Out of here. Now!"

The rest of the cops rushed past Bec and tackled Lane, Kris, and Vic as they tried to run further into the passageway. Bec stumbled along behind a man she thought of as an uncle, unable to pull free of his iron grip. All thoughts of freedom after finding proof of her innocence fled her numb brain.

Once outside, Mike sat Bec far from her friends. She stared at the people she'd trusted all her life. Because of her, they faced the loss of their freedom.

"None of you talk to each other," Mike said. "We're going to take this one person at a time. I don't want to hear what someone told you. I don't want speculation. Just what you know. Then we'll figure out where we go from there."

"Then you don't have to talk to anyone else," Bec said. "But we really need to get out of here, Uncle Mike."

"You won't get on my good side by calling me Uncle," Mike said.

"You have a lot of explaining to do, Bec. Why didn't you call us right away? Why did you run?"

She lifted her frightened eyes to his furious face and explained how she came to be in Lane's Mustang, behind the wheel. That was the one part of the story everyone would have a hard time believing. Lane never let anyone else drive his precious muscle car. His dad had given it to him as a graduation gift, and the restored classic car was Lane's pride and joy.

"I really, really, thought Lane wanted me to help him check the taillights," Bec said in a pleading voice. "But when I figured out what was happening, I tried to get out. Lane shoved a gun into my ribs."

"Better believe it," Jack shouted. "She has the beginnings of a bruise on her ribs. And it looks exactly like a muzzle."

"Is that true?" Mike speared Bec in place with a ferocious glare. His coffee-dark skin glistened with sweat. "Don't bother lying, Bec. I can always tell when you are."

Bec nodded. "Lane shoved me out on the side of the highway, Uncle Mike. He didn't even slow down." She pointed at her mud-smeared shorts. "See?"

"I see." Mike held out a massive hand. "Let me see that bruise."

Some of Bec's worry eased when Mike hissed in anger at the sight of the bruise. Before he had a chance to say anything, the cops came out of the passageway with Lane, Kris, and Vic.

"It was all her idea!" Lane yelled. "Don't believe that bitch. She set it up and laughed about the whole thing!"

"I'd believe you, Miller, but there's just one little problem," Mike said. "You shouldn't have shoved a gun into her ribs. And you shouldn't have cut off that truck driver. After a good long interview, he decided it was kind of strange seeing some guy with one arm cocked at an angle against the side of a girl and sitting practically on top of her. We'd already decided Bec didn't rob the store."

Bec sat on the spongy ground in relief. All her worries for nothing. She watched as Lane, Kris, and Vic protested their innocence while the cops shoved them into separate patrol cars. A nervous laugh pushed out of her throat and her crew looked at her as if she'd gone mental.

"What's so funny?" Dy asked.

"All we wanted was to find a clue to the Tremaine fortune," Bec said.

"Keisha will go nuts once she hears what we really did."

"You might have a chance to 'find' that fortune." Bec's dad crouched in front of her. "We saw what looks like an old trunk in that cave. But until I know you're okay, you don't get to find out for sure."

"I'm okay, Dad." Bec hugged her dad. "And I really mean that. I'm okay now. I wasn't until Uncle Mike yelled at Lane. Why didn't you tell me in the cave?"

"Because I was ready to ground you for the rest of your life for scaring me so badly," Dad admitted. "I know you're nineteen and ready to go to college, but I always thought you'd come to me if you were in trouble."

"I'm sorry." She scrambled to her feet. "Can we look at that trunk now?"

"Yes." Dad hugged her. "Be careful. I see wild chamomile all over."

"We know." Bec took off with her friends.

A cop escorted them back to the cave and then moved into another passageway. Bec stared at the ancient trunk that was set against a wall and held her breath. After all they'd gone through, it couldn't happen this easily.

"Who opens the trunk?" the cop asked.

"Bec," her friends said.

"She earned it," Ev said as he walked alongside Bec to the trunk.

"Together," Bec said. "We'll do it together."

Their hands side by side, Bec and Ev undid the straps and lifted the lid of the trunk. Bundles and bundles of very old-looking money were stacked to the top of the trunk.

"OMG!" Bec said in a breathy whisper. "We found more than a clue. This is the Tremaine fortune!"

For one very crazy second, she considered changing her college major from business management to police science. Then she shook her head and let the guys muscle the trunk outside. Two mysteries solved in one day were more than enough for her.

KC Sprayberry loves reading, but not as much as she loves writing stories for young adults and middle-graders. Her interest in telling her stories goes back to her high school years, where she excelled in any and all writing classes. After a move to the northwest area of Georgia, she dove into this pursuit full-time while raising her children. While she spends many days researching areas of interest, she also loves photography and often uses it as a way to integrate scenery into her work.

Truth and Consequences
by Barb Goffman

"We discussed prostitution, adultery, and drug use in school today," I announced at dinner. "Did you know they're victimless crimes?"

My mother nearly choked on her green beans. "You what?"

"It was all Andy Telwacht's fault. He and Robbie Winters did their oral debate in social studies on marijuana. Robbie called it a gateway drug and said people should go to jail for a long time for using it. Then Andy said that smoking pot didn't hurt anyone, and it should be legal here in Illinois just like it is in Europe!"

Dad's eyes bugged out while Mom's face turned a deep red. Boy, I loved to get them going.

"You know how Mr. Carracio always tells us to think for ourselves?" I went on. "So we got into this big debate about whether marijuana is dangerous. Bonnie Kingman said it's not, that it's just like prostitution and adultery. If everyone's a consenting adult, what's the problem? I kind of think she's right."

Mom slapped the tabletop so hard, my plate of chicken bounced. "This is what we get for spending our hard-earned money on that fancy private school."

She scowled and wagged her finger at me. "You listen to me, Cara. Drug use, prostitution, and adultery are *not* victimless crimes. People get hurt in ways you can't even begin to fathom when you're fourteen years old. If you even think about doing drugs and I find out about it—and believe me, I will—you will rue the day."

I rolled my eyes. *Rue the day*. Mom was so melodramatic.

• • •

An hour later, Dad poked his head in my room. His curly brown hair fell across his forehead, covering his eyebrows. He looked so dorky. I tugged off my iPod earbuds.

"Mom and I are going to the supermarket," he said. "She wants ice cream. I'll turn on the alarm on the way out."

"Okay," I said. "See you later."

I tried to play it cool, but I was psyched. Now I could ditch my algebra homework for something far more important: searching for my Christmas presents. Ten days till Christmas. No way I could wait that long to see what this year's haul would be. Over the last week, I'd hunted around the house for my gifts. I'd only found one: a black and gray Dooney & Bourke wristlet buried in a Tupperware container. Mom's been real sneaky about hiding my presents since fifth grade, when she caught me searching for them. Boy, had she yelled that day.

"Cara Beth Holloway, what do you think you're doing?"

I was elbow-deep in her underwear drawer. What did she think I was doing?

"You get out of this room right now, young lady. Snooping can be dangerous business."

Yeah, right. I couldn't imagine what I might possibly discover that would be *dangerous*. My parents simply weren't that interesting.

Now, with them out for probably an hour, I concentrated my search on their bedroom. Every nook and cranny had to be systematically examined. Mom's stealth knew no bounds.

Unfortunately, after a half hour, I still hadn't found anything meant for me. Dad had apparently bought cruise tickets for him and Mom (which meant—please no—that my grandparents would come to watch me while they were gone). Where was my stuff? I really wanted that new phone Kim got for her birthday. It's tiny. It could be hidden anywhere.

I decided to hit the closet by the front door. I hadn't checked there yet. I rifled through every pocket of every coat. Nothing. Then I reached down to the snow shoes we kept in the back of the closet. Maybe Mom had slipped something inside one of them.

I was on my knees when I heard keys in the front door. Oh, no! I quickly snuggled back behind the coats and had almost pulled the closet door shut when Mom and Dad came in. I crooked my head sideways, peering through the crack.

"You really think she'll like them?" Mom whispered, holding a bag from Jake, one of the hottest stores here in Winnetka.

I nearly hyperventilated. My boots! They had to be the black suede boots I wanted!

"Of course she'll like them," Dad said. "She has the same expensive tastes you do, and these boots cost a fortune."

He pulled the closet door open, and I nearly hyperventilated again.

How would I explain hiding in the closet? If they caught me, Mom might just return the boots to teach me a lesson. She loved doing things like that. I held my breath and tried not to move as Dad reached in and grabbed a hanger.

"Oh, before I forget," Mom said.

Dad looked over his shoulder.

"The coat I ordered for Cara has come in," Mom said. "I need you to pick it up tomorrow."

Coat? What coat?

Dad shoved his jacket in the closet and turned, shaking his head back and forth like he always does when he starts getting aggravated. "Why can't you do it?"

I took a breath as quietly as possible as Dad snatched another hanger and shoved Mom's fur-trimmed coat on the rack. It pushed up against my nose, which began tickling.

"Why can't *I* do it?" Mom said. "Because I have a hair appointment, Christmas is right around the corner, and the store's at Northbrook Court. You'll be heading that way anyway. Won't you?" Mom's tone made clear she knew the answer was yes.

I swallowed hard, trying to smother the sneeze that now desperately wanted out.

"You know how limited my time is on Saturdays," Dad said. "And I won't be able to go at all next weekend, what with the relatives coming to visit."

"I don't want to hear it, Bill. Cara never gets any of your time on Saturday afternoons. This is the least you can do for her."

If I didn't know better, I'd think they were drawing out this conversation to make me suffer. Heck, maybe they were.

"Fine," Dad said, shutting the closet door. "I've got to get this ice cream into the freezer before it melts."

I waited a few seconds, wrinkling and rubbing my nose, then let out a huge breath. That was close. I waited another thirty seconds before inching the door open. The coast was clear.

As I snuck back to my room, I wondered yet again what kept Dad busy each Saturday. He always left around lunchtime to "run errands" and came home hours later with a bag of bagels and the *Chicago Tribune*. I asked to go along once when I was little, but he said no, that he had important, secret work to do. I'd decided then that he was a spy. But of course that couldn't be true. No way Dad could fix people's teeth during the week and be a spy on the weekends. And I knew he really was a dentist. I'd suffered in his chair more than once.

So what was this important, secret work? And why would it piss off Mom? My snooping gene in overdrive, I decided I finally had to find out. Besides, it might give me the chance to check out my new coat at the same time. Maybe it was suede, too, and matched my boots!

A knock on my bedroom door interrupted my coat fantasy. "Come in."

"Just wanted to let you know that we're home, honey," Mom said, leaning against the door frame. "We bought some of your favorite strawberry ice cream, in case you want any."

"Yum! Thanks. Hey, I made plans to go over to Kim's tomorrow. FYI."

"Okay. Do you want a ride?"

"No. It's just a few blocks. The exercise will be good for me. I can work off the ice cream I'm going to eat."

Mom smiled. "Sweet dreams, then. I'm getting in bed with my ice cream and my *People* magazine."

Once I heard her bedroom door close, I called my best friend, Kim. She agreed to be my cover for the next day, after making me promise to give her all the details of my spy mission.

With a plan in place, I sat at the kitchen table with a small dish of ice cream and my algebra homework. Dad always pushed me to get my assignments done Friday night, so I wouldn't have to worry about them all weekend long. I tried to finish the math, but I honestly couldn't care less about figuring out what X stood for. I had a bigger puzzle on my mind.

• • •

My alarm woke me at 11 o'clock the next morning. Most weekend days, I sleep till noon. While I hated giving up my catch-up sleep—on school days I have to get up at the obscene hour of six—satisfying my curiosity would be worth it. I took a quick, twenty-minute shower, dressed, blew my hair dry, grabbed some PowerBars, and headed out.

But instead of walking over to Kim's, I got in the back of Dad's blue Lexus and burrowed under the old blanket on the backseat. Mom was going through "the change," and sometimes she'd get really hot and switch on the car air conditioner, even if it was twenty degrees outside! So Dad left a blanket on the backseat for me to use during family car rides.

I texted with Kim for a few minutes. When I heard Dad's keys jingling, I jammed the phone's off button, plunged onto the floor behind Dad's seat, and focused on staying still and breathing lightly. I prayed the crumpled blanket didn't attract Dad's attention.

Moments later, Dad climbed behind the wheel, turned on the radio, and off we went. He hadn't noticed me. Score!

We drove for about fifteen minutes, accompanied by a Beatles marathon. (Could my dad be more lame?) I could tell when we reached the mall because Dad started muttering about the traffic and all the holiday shoppers. It sounded like he circled a bit before he finally he found a spot and headed in. I waited a few seconds after he left the car to throw off the blanket and peek out the window. He'd parked by the movie theater. That would mean my coat might come from Abercrombie & Fitch. Or Ann Taylor. Did they sell coats? Or…please, please, please… maybe Mom bought me a coat from CUSP. It's the coolest store *ever*.

I nibbled on a PowerBar while I kept my eyes trained on the mall entrance. Finally, about ten minutes later, Dad came out with a bag from … oh my God! CUSP! My life couldn't get any better. Any coat from CUSP would be totally fab. My friends would be so jealous!

I curled up under the blanket again just before Dad got in the car and tossed the CUSP bag on the front passenger seat. Soon we were off again. I meant to pay attention to where we were going, but I kept thinking about ways I could peek at my coat. I couldn't stand waiting nine more days.

Maybe twenty minutes later, the car stopped again. Dad got out, and it sounded like he lifted the trunk lid, then slammed it shut. When he didn't get back in the car, I slipped the blanket off my head and brushed my hair from my face. Jeez, it had gotten hot under there. I glanced out the window. We were in a townhouse complex with bare trees surrounding the parking lot. Dad was heading for an end unit, carrying some wrapped gifts.

What kind of errand was this?

I noticed the CUSP bag still on the front passenger seat and shifted toward it while I kept my eyes on Dad. He reached the door, pulled out a key, and let himself in.

What the...?

The coat could wait. I shot out of the car, dashed to the house's front window, and on tippy-toes peered inside. A woman with long blond hair was putting most of Dad's gifts under a stubby Christmas tree with white lights. And there was Dad, hugging some kid with curly brown hair.

The kid seemed a few years younger than me and kind of looked familiar. Dad handed him one of the gifts; he tore it open and smiled. I sucked in my breath when he did, because I knew that smile. Dad's smile. The kid hugged him again, and even though I couldn't read lips very well, the kid's next words clearly were, "Thanks, Daddy."

A brother?

I had a brother?

I spun away from the window and rubbed my hand over my face. Dad wasn't a spy. He was a bigamist. Or an adulterer. Or something else awful. I'd always wanted a brother or sister, but not like this. I'd have to tell Mom. I sagged against the building. Wait. Mom must already know. She knows how Dad leaves every Saturday. That's what they argued about last night.

I slid down against the side of the house. The aluminum siding's coldness seeped straight through my jacket, into my bones. This couldn't be happening. I live in Winnetka. In a nice house. With my parents. Both of them. We're a normal family. No problems. And Christmas is coming. I'm going to get great gifts. Like every year. No way Dad is leading a double life. No way he has another kid. I'm his kid. His only kid. I must have made a mistake.

I scrambled up, went to the door, and knocked before I lost my nerve. The blond woman opened the door a moment later and gasped. Then Dad gasped, too.

"Who's that girl, Daddy?" the kid asked.

Wow. I wasn't the only one who'd been lied to.

"Cara!" Dad rushed to the door. "What are you doing here?"

I was breathing heavily. "I wanted to see my coat and find out where you went all the time, so I hid in the backseat. I wanted to be in on the big secret. Please tell me this is all a joke, Dad. Right? You're his Big

Brother or something like that? Right? We learned about that in school. That's a really nice thing to do. Or you're here doing community service. Dental house calls? Is that it? There's got to be an explanation."

I was talking too fast. Maybe if I kept talking, I'd come up with a good reason why this was happening.

Dad grabbed my arms. "Cara, calm down." He shook me a little until I focused on him. "You weren't supposed to find out this way. Your mother and I decided to wait until you were older. Until you could handle it."

"Handle what?" It took all my strength not to cry. "What's going on?"

Eyes darting between me and the kid, Dad appeared on the verge of tears, too. He pulled me toward the couch set against the wall, then waved the kid over to us. His hair was the same shade of brown as Dad's. And mine.

Chin quivering, Dad focused on me. "Cara, this is your brother, Michael." He turned to the kid. "Michael ... you have a big sister. Her name is Cara."

The kid looked as freaked out as I felt.

"What?" The kid whipped his head back and forth between Dad and the blond lady. "Mommy, what's Daddy mean? A sister? I don't get it."

Snooping can be dangerous business. Mom's voice echoed in my head.

The blond woman came over and held out her hand. "Michael, let's go to your room so I can explain some things." Her voice shook a little.

The kid turned and stared at me for a minute, then took her hand. As they headed down a hallway, I noticed a bunch of pictures on the wall, including one of Dad and the kid. Swallowing hard, I turned my attention to the faded blue and yellow flower-print on the couch until Dad lifted my chin with his finger.

"Your mom and I had some problems when you were little. And I made some mistakes. Jocelyn," he nodded toward the bedroom, "used to be my dental hygienist." Dad sighed. "I guess you're old enough to hear this now...Well, we had an affair." He scrunched his eyes closed for a second and shook his head. "It didn't last very long. I realized how much I love your mom and broke it off, but by then Michael was on the way."

I didn't want to know about this. I kept thinking about my new coat and boots. If I kept thinking about them, surely this would all go away.

"It took a long time for your mom to forgive me," Dad continued. "And she's been very supportive all these years, letting me come here every Saturday to spend time with your brother. He's a great kid. You're going to love him."

Love him? I didn't even know him.

Lots of my friends' parents were divorced, but I'd never worried about that. I thought Mom and Dad were happy. But how happy could they be with this big secret in their lives? It must be so hard on Mom knowing Dad spends every Saturday with this other family. With this woman that he…I shook my head. I couldn't go there. How could Dad have this other life all these years and I never knew? How could he have done this to Mom? To us?

And Mom. My God. How could she have accepted this? How could she have forgiven him? How could I?

"You're growing up, Cara," Dad said. "You're fourteen now. It's time you learned life isn't always nice and tidy. But we can make this work." He paused. "How I'm going to explain this to your mother is another story."

I stared at him, my eyes watering. What would I tell Kim? I'd have to make something up. She couldn't know. No one could know. It's one thing for parents to divorce, marry other people, and then have more kids. But to have an affair and a child like this? And to hide it for years? Everyone would talk about me if they knew. All the kids would laugh or point or whisper.

"Please, honey. It's nearly Christmas. If you could try to accept your brother, it would be the best present in the world to me."

My heart said no, but I felt my head nodding yes. Dad hugged me.

"Thank you, Cara. This is going to work out. You'll see. No more secrets. Finally I'll be able to spend time with you and Michael together as a family. "

Great, family togetherness with a stranger.

I laid my head on Dad's shoulder and felt the first tears slide from my eyes as I tried to make sense of it all. Unbelievable that just a half hour before, a new suede coat and boots had me on top of the world.

Bonnie Kingman didn't know *what* she was talking about. Mom was right: there's no such thing as a victimless crime.

What a crock.

Barb Goffman is a short-story mystery author whose work tends to focus on families. Twice nominated for the Agatha Award, she is a member of the national board of Sisters in Crime, a co-coordinating editor of *Chesapeake Crimes: They Had It Comin'* and the forthcoming *Chesapeake Crimes: This Job is Murder*, and is program chair of the Malice Domestic mystery convention. She lives in Virginia with her miracle dog, Scout (a three-time cancer survivor!). You can learn more about her at barbgoffman.com.

Frost

by Melanie Cummins

It snowed the night he was released from prison. The night I had planned to murder him…

When I found out they were setting him free, I admit, I snapped. I wasn't supposed to know he was out. His freedom was a military secret that had somehow seeped through the cracks and reached me. Back in the day, he had been a Navy SEAL, a good one, too. He had been admired by his comrades as a great leader.

Besides being a spirited petty officer, he was a trained killer, which came in handy when he stole the lives of everyone I ever loved.

On this night, this beautiful night, I hid in the shadows, shaking from the chill of the lightly falling snow. When the police brought him to the prison door, I saw his black suit dotted with white crystals. His handcuffs clanged together as they were removed.

He stepped out into the moonlight, letting the outside world see his face. He had one of those faces that could have made him famous— fascinating blue eyes, strong cheekbones, and soft lips. Three years ago, he had chosen to cover that face with a leather mask and use his invisibility to take lives.

He had meant to kill me too; I saw it in the vulnerable part of his eyes. I was younger than him, fifteen at the time. His mask had fallen off in the fight with my father. He looked into my eyes and froze, the knife clenched in his hand. I told him to do it, to kill me, with a shaky voice.

We stared into each other's eyes as he hovered over me. I didn't dare scream. There was a strange moment of connection when I reached up and touched the side of his face, tracing a tear that had fallen down his cheek. He abandoned the knife and placed his hand over mine. My entire body was trembling; my heart nearly thumping out of my body. He told me that he wasn't going to hurt me, that I was in shock, but that I was going to be okay. He tried to escape, but was a moment too late.

The cops came and almost ended his life then and there. He gave himself up to them, ready for incarceration. And there I was, sitting in a circle of bodies. I wished that he had taken my life, too. One of the cops tried to speak to me. I don't remember what happened over the next few hours, only that I felt entirely lifeless.

I shook off the memory and brought my mind back to the present.

He stood there, reveling in the crisp air. From his cautiousness, I felt as though he knew I was there. His face had hardened over the three years he had been locked up, and tattoos now ran along his neck. Dusting off his jacket, he shivered in the cold breeze. He looked up in the black sky as if it were the most amazing sight in the world.

"Thanks, Commander." I heard his voice for the first time in years. Sure, I've played his last words over and over in my head, losing myself in them, but in person, they chilled me to the bone. His voice had haunted me every night for three years. Now I was ready to let him go. To end his life.

He walked over to the car parked in front of him and pressed his gloved hand against the roof. "Just as I left her. Perfect."

The Commander stood tall, not the least bit unnerved. I'd seen him before, three years ago. He had waited at the front door, grief splashed across his face. I always thought that soldiers in uniform had such prestige. The Commander seemed so graceful in front of me while his lips moved in an apology. His stance now was the same. "Thank you for your service to your country. You know where you're staying tonight. We'll pick you up at o-six-hundred tomorrow morning. You vanish, we'll finish the job. You and I both don't want to hurt that young girl, so I sincerely hope you keep your promise."

"My promise is as good as gold. See you then, Commander." They saluted each other.

I was so entranced, I barely noticed the Commander drive away into the silent night. The prison guard stared straight ahead, almost militant, waiting for my attacker to get in his car.

"You look perfect, Kate," he said, just loud enough for me to hear.

My heart, already flying, skipped a beat. He couldn't have seen me. I was hidden well enough to be invisible even to the guards.

It took me a moment to realize he was speaking to his car.

The car rumbled as the engine warmed up. He took off down the road, glancing back only once to wave at the guards. The moment they saw the wave, they nodded and headed indoors.

I waited a second or two before returning to my car down the road.

As I unlocked the door, I realized I should have worn a warmer coat. My skin was numb and my feet kept sinking into this soft, bitterly cold snow.

I slid into my car and cranked the heater up full blast, hoping to ward off the shivers. The car's lights were off. This would be a slow but steady stalking. I would be dead if he knew I was following him.

Guided only by the soft moonlight, he sped through the winding roads with precision. I followed, swallowing the torment raging in my body. I needed him gone so that my head would be quiet. I could not handle one more night of my mind endlessly repeating his words.

When I received the call informing me of his impending release, it almost broke me. He had only served three years. That would never be enough for what he had done to my family.

He took a quick turn, heading up a winding trail. Since I was not such a great driver, my little Volkswagen was in danger of crashing in the thick snow. I parked it in the shadows, quietly got out, and followed him up the mountain on foot. It was quite a long way up, filled with sharp boulders on every side. If I tripped, it would be a long, cold, hazardous fall. I tried not to think of it as I pushed my way up the snowy cliff. When I reached the halfway mark, there was a creaking, rusted sign that said simply, "Dead Man's Bend."

As my body shivered, I began to wish I'd never gotten that phone call the previous week. The little peace that I had in my life had been severed by the man's words. "He's getting out, the first of December," he had said. "Military orders." And then he had hung up. I had dialed back, determined to get a response. Of course there was no answer. I had my information, and I made the decision to act on it, whether or not death was imminent.

Up at the top, I let my body relax. If the circumstances had been different, I would have been at peace up here on the plateau. The safe house was tucked on top of the mountain, entirely invisible to anyone in the surrounding area.

A chill came over me as the wind picked up. My face was the coldest part of my body. I reached in my pocket and pulled out the godforsaken mask he had worn. The obsessive part of me had kept it in case I ever confronted him.

It was gruesome but warm. At least my face would be saved from frostbite. I could smell remnants of him in that mask, the musk and the sweat. After a few moments of breathing that in, I decided I would rather have a numb face. I pulled the mask down so that it would at least shield my neck from the wind.

It was then I noticed his empty car and the small light shining in the corner of the cabin.

Now I was concerned with *how* I would kill him. Electrocution? Fire? I looked down at the gun I had brought. That might do the trick. But how satisfying would it be? Would I be able to do this? Would I freeze up the moment I was face-to-face with him, just as he had with me?

Would I end up in jail, where he belonged? I never understood why he killed them and why he saved me. Sure, my family had secrets, but I had never witnessed them doing anything illegal, no matter what the military said.

I was crying now. My face was burning, my nose was running, and my body was exhausted. I wasn't sure I could complete this task without ruining myself more than I already had.

But before I could contemplate an exit strategy, he strolled out the front door. He stood there, gazing into the distance, once again mesmerized by the outside world. Anyone who saw him could see the love affair he had with the nature around him, probably caused by his lack of scenery over the years.

I was in plain sight. One quick look to the left, and I would be discovered. That very fact kept me frozen in place.

Ten minutes passed until his eyes shifted my way. My body would not move no matter how much as I willed it to.

His eyes were filled with nothing but pity. He moved toward me, undeterred by the gun in my hand. "Who told you?"

I didn't dare answer.

He took another step forward, and when he did, I took out my gun and shot. Being the terrible shot that I am, I injured the snow, not him. I shot again, hitting the cabin this time. Glass shattered as the bullet broke a window.

Even though I didn't hit him, it felt good to see some fear in his eyes. I smiled despite the situation. "Put the gun down, Katie." He stood close, too close, and pressed his hand against my gun. "You came to kill me?"

he asked, nearly as quiet as the falling snow.

"I came to find answers. I came to stop being scared to sleep at night."

"You don't look scared." His eyes were trained on the mask around my neck.

If I ran, he would have caught me. If I tried to shoot him, he would have shot me first. So I stalled.

"The war needs you, huh?"

"The government pardoned me. They need the best of the best right now."

"Then why was it a secret?"

"Nobody likes the publicity of a government scandal." He lifted his hand and touched the side of my face, causing me to shake more than I already was. "You cold? The cabin's warm."

"You think I'm that stupid?" I choked out. "I'd rather freeze to death."

"Suit yourself," he said, beginning a walk back to the cabin.

It took all I had, but I managed to ask, "Why didn't you kill me?"

That stopped him in his tracks. "You weren't part of the deal. You didn't do anything."

"*Neither did they!*" I shouted, as years of pent-up anger billowed out. My voice carried over the trees around us, bouncing off the mountains.

He met my eyes again. "That's what you want to believe."

"That was my family," I spat. "They were innocent human beings and you ripped them apart without a second thought. Don't tell me it was justified. War should never be justified when it tears families apart."

He stomped over to me, fury lighting up his eyes. "I was a soldier, Katie. Bad stuff happens. Of course it shouldn't be justified, but that's the way it was. I was given orders, I carried them out."

The cold got worse as the night grew darker, but the adrenaline rush kept my body warm enough. "Orders? You were *ordered* to kill them?"

He shook his head in disbelief. "You don't want to know how corrupt your family was."

I used the little strength I had left to push him away from me. "Tell me."

Before I knew it, his arms were keeping me in place. He held me still even though I fought back. "Katie, calm down," he said. "They were soldier patrollers. We didn't catch on for a while, because it seemed as though they were helping out the wounded guys. But they were just pretending. They were taking the wounded in and then torturing them until they died, or until they gave them the information they were searching for."

I'd heard hints of this story before, lies told by those on the military side. I knew my parents. I *loved* my parents. They died in his arms. His nefarious actions stole their future away from them. I needed him to pay for what I lost that day.

"Stop lying," I said. I couldn't stop the tears now. "Justice was served, at least until today. You went to jail for this."

"Because nobody believed me," he said. "It was a price I paid. My commander couldn't give himself up or it would have compromised the team. So I was the good soldier and let them incarcerate me."

"You should have killed me," I said. "You should have cleaned up your mess."

"You're not the only one who suffered," he said.

"Finish your orders. I've been tortured for three years. I'd rather be free than be tortured any longer."

The anger in his face faded to shame. "I'm not going to hurt you, Katie."

His words, a slight repeat of our first encounter, caused me to push him one more time. But this time he lost his footing. After grasping in the air for something to hold on to, he realized he was on the edge. He slid a few inches, and instinct made me reach out. That stupid decision caused me to lose my footing as well.

He reached for me, perhaps trying to steady me, but we were already tumbling through the snow. We gained speed faster than I thought was possible, even though he kept a strong grip on my arm all the way down. Those seconds felt like hours, but time halted when we were stopped by a thump and a crunching of bones.

My bones.

My whimpering grew loud. His body was slumped nearby. He stirred. Shaking off the pain, he limped over to me. He had a twisted ankle and a torn-up arm, courtesy of the trees.

"Jack," I cried out, saying his name for the first time in my life. "Jack, I can't move. My legs."

I glanced down and watched my pants slowly grow dark with blood, and strong emotion came over his face.

He tried to pick me up, but my screeching stopped him from moving me any further. "I need to get you back to the cabin," he said. "You need to be strong."

My eye were blurry from tears and snowflakes. I shook my head. "I guess I'm the one dying, huh? You win again." I continued to sob, just about the only thing I was useful for at that moment. I wanted to laugh this situation away and turn back time to when life was easier. The way it looked, I was the one dying at the bottom of the mountain.

Jack moved close to me and slid off his jacket. The cold reached his body right away. He placed the jacket around me with a sigh. "You're gonna kill both of us, you know that, right?"

"Do you have a cell phone on you?"

"I've been in jail for three years. What about you?"

"I didn't think I'd need it. I figured tonight wouldn't end well."

Jack pulled me toward him so that I was staring into his face. As difficult as it was, I kept a constant watch on him.

"We are not going to die here, okay? You're going to let me pull you up to the house."

I reached for my gun, still in my pocket, and lifted it up. I wasn't sure who I was going to kill, him or myself, but Jack snatched it and let it tumble down the mountain before I could make that decision.

"Just go," I said. "Get to town and get help."

"I'm not leaving you lying next to this tree with a bunch of broken bones. You'll freeze to death before I even get there."

He was as close as he could get, spreading his body heat to me. I was so cold, but I kept my eyes open so I could keep watching him.

"You're getting up that mountain. We aren't giving up now." He pushed himself off the ground and held out his hand. "Trust me, even if it's for the last time in your life."

I shook my head.

Not amused, he bent down and took me in his arms. This time he didn't put me down, no matter how loud I yelled. "I've been in prison for a while. I can deal with you screaming all the way up to the mountain."

Sure, there was a harshness in his voice. But somewhere, deep inside, I could tell that he cared. This made me relax and lean into him, hoping that we would make it to the warm cabin.

He was only a few feet up before he slowed down. I looked up at him and saw that he was paling from the temperature. My legs ached with every long step of his. Finally, as the cabin came into view, he set me back down on the snow and lay down in it. He couldn't make it any farther.

"I know you hate me," he said. "And you will for the rest of your life. But just know that I would never murder innocent people. I'm not proud of what I did, but I'm glad that I helped the people I did, Katie."

He went silent. I tried to wake him up with a few punches. "Jack?" He was still breathing, but the cold had gotten to him. Now I had to make the most difficult decision of my life. I could try to crawl to the cabin and try to get warm. I could stay here with him and hope that the commander would come early. Or I could try to pull him to the cabin, probably the most difficult task of all.

I looked up in the sky and noticed that the sun wasn't coming up anytime soon. Thousands of stars shimmered down on me, seeming to tell me what to do.

Without warmth, he would fall into hypothermia and die. And I now knew that coming here with a gun was a mistake. I was never going to kill him. I wanted justice to either prove him a criminal or to set us both free. Even though I was overwhelmed, I knew that I could not let him die without knowing the truth.

Despite my reservations, I forced myself to tug at his arms. His body was warm, and he stirred as I pulled him up. I cried softly in the falling snow as I rocked my hips up and down, trying to use rocks as leverage. I wanted to let him go as the pain intensified, but the strongest part of me kept a solid grasp on his arms.

It was a small miracle, but we reached the door of the cabin. Jack woke. He shoved the door open and pulled me inside.

There were problems with the cabin. For one, the heater was pretty much shot. Cold air kept rushing in through the window that I had shot out. And the blizzard had knocked the telephone out. I kept fading away and then coming back, my energy dissipating by the second. "Kate," he would say every time I lost consciousness, "Wake up, my Katie."

The last time I saw his face was when he set me on the couch and placed his palm on my wet cheek.

And the last sound I would ever hear from him was my own name, uttered by his cold, cracked lips.

• • •

The commander found me in the morning, o-six-hundred on the dot. I say *me* because Jack was gone. When I woke up, I was being loaded in the ambulance. When I saw the Commander, I begged to know where Jack was. He pretended as though he didn't know what I was talking about. His facade was good enough to make me doubt that I had seen Jack at all.

I knew in my heart it was true. What happened on the mountain would change my views about everything that had happened to me. I promised myself to investigate and find the truth, with or without justice.

There was no sign of him. No tracks, no DNA. The cabin was empty of everything except for an old lantern. I even went to the jail where he had been held, but they refused to give me any information. The jacket that Jack had wrapped me in was gone when I woke up. So was the mask. He had simply vanished.

Had they carried his dead body off, a secret the commander would take to the grave?

Part of me will not accept this.

I believe Jack is still out there, watching me from the shadows.

Waiting for me to find him again.

Melanie Cummins is a busy college student and a full-time writer. When she's not typing away late at night, she studies criminal justice at the University of West Florida. While Melanie adores writing short stories, her true love lies in writing thrillers.

Our Judges

Our Book Blogger Panel

Danielle Smith, aka The1stdaughter from the children's book review site There's A Book, is a reader, reviewer, and writer of books of all varieties.

Gina Reba is the "insatiable reader" behind the site Satisfaction for Insatiable Readers. Gina is an avid reader, reviewer, and general lover of the written word.

Kristina Guidroz is also known as the Cajun Book Lady on the site where she reviews her favorite genres: young adult, paranormal/fantasy, romance, and horror.

Our Teen Panel

Caleb G is a sophomore honors student and an avid reader. His shelves are full of fantasy and science fiction books, which inspire his own writing.

Katy H is a senior honors student who always has a book in one hand and two more on her TBR pile. She is a cheerleader and is looking forward to starting college in the fall.

Connor M is a seventh-grader. He is an avid reader, soccer player, video game fanatic, Boy Scout, and band student, and he spends his spare time with friends and family.

Jessica G is a freshman and an avid reader who loves paranormal, mystery, thrillers and anything else she can get her hands on.

Madison M will be attending an all-girl high school next fall. Her friends call her room "the library" because she has so many books. She plays soccer and enjoys teasing her younger brothers.

Our Editorial Review Panel

Erica Sommer Karcher works for Baker & Taylor's Children's and Teens Services and writes reviews for Visual Bookshelf.

Joan Apgar recently retired after twenty-six years at a major book wholesaler. She spent fifteen of those years as a children's and YA book buyer.

Ellen Myrick has over two decades of experience in the children's and YA book field. She worked at the largest book wholesaler in the United States and now runs Myrick Marketing & Media LLC.

www.ingramcontent.com/pod-product-compliance
Lightning Source LLC
Chambersburg PA
CBHW071305130626
46556CB00003B/1477